Covered In Sin

An Inspirational Urban Drama

by

Aleta

Copyright page

Covered In Sin

Contents

I Prayed For This...

Multiple times I have stood in church or was on my knees praying in the spirit for this story to do what God intended it to do. And each time I prayed I saw a vision of a young lady holding her pillow crying. I began to pray that she picks the book up and when she reads it she will learn God is real and right where she is. I pray for you all boy and girl, lady and man. Healed human and unhealed human. *I pray Covered in Sin reveals things to you that will remove anything that is blocking and or hindering you in life, but most of all I pray that you will utterly understand that God is with you and that he isn't far at all. Amen.*

Originally this was to be one book but now its two. In part one you will see the foundation setup and in part 2 everything will end as it should. I do have the ending in mind but God is in control so we shall see what happens in the last installment.

A message from the author

Hey guys, thank you for your interest in this title. To my seasoned supporters I thank you for your continued love and support and to my first timers, I thank you for allowing my creativity into your soul.

After 13 years I have retired as an Urban Fiction Hood/Street author and am now embarking on a new journey! I present a new genre- one I'd like to say I created "Inspirational Urban Drama with a Christian Twist."

When I began my journey as an author in April 2010 I let the world know that I was writing to entertain and inspire. My goal was to speak the language of my targeted audience while delivering a message that will hopefully introduce them or pull them close to Christ and then they will understand the street life ain't it. I wanted my readers to know that Jesus is the reason why a lot of us are still alive, beat that case, survived that childhood and is striving for greatness. And I still pray that something I say, write, and or. Produce will do just that.

My debut novel In Da Hood and now movie is where I started. By the way, the book is more in depth than the movie that was produced 12 years later. After the first book I forgot my purpose and ended up writing drama after drama. It did more than well on the market. Eventually, I no longer wrote from passion or fun but with the hopes of making the money I had made years prior. My father passed, the next year my grandmother, and then soon after my husband went back to prison. Here I was depressed again but this time I did not have my father as a support system until I figured it out. So much I must share but I will in memoir or another non-fiction book.

   October 2022 I visited my now church home. The prophet spoke on purpose and if our purpose is to uplift God. During the service God revealed to me why it was so hard for me to write urban fiction- why it seemed so forced. Basically, I forgot my purpose and the time was to get back on track.

My Inspirational Urban Dramas will be the first book that many will read and feel like there is hope. Many will say, now someone understands me. There will be dozens who will realize God isn't far but right with us and they can overcome all afflictions through Christ Jesus who strengthens us.

   I thank God for using me as a vessel and no man or woman will take away or make me feel as though I do not hear direct from God through him or my Angels. The delivery isn't for ALL humans but for those God is using me to reach. In all your getting get an understanding and remember, WE ARE NOT GOD- I do not care how you think I am to minister so, save yourself time and leave it off the reviews- I do not care- I Write for JESUS. This is my platform.

Don't forget your review.

Covered In Sin

An Inspirational Urban Drama

Chapter One:
ME AGAINST THE WORLD, TUPAC

The room reeked of Bengay and the Elizabeth Taylor fragrance White Diamonds. Winter hated her grandmother's signature scent. It smelled up the entire apartment and always made her feel icky on the inside, but at such a young age, she could not identify the heaviness and uncertainty she felt when her grandmother was around. So, she associated the feeling with the scent. However, when she smelled it a couple of hours ago, she was grateful; she welcomed it. Someone was home to rescue her from her nightmare.

Standing in front of her as she sat on the pissy mattress, Winter's grandmother scolded her, "Big-lip, ugly little girl, ain't no man ever gonna want to be with you. You're a troublemaker just like your old mama was."

Sweets cursed her granddaughter like she was the scum of the earth. The disgusted look on her face was almost as hurtful as the names she called her. She had not seen the evil side of her grandmother until that very moment, but those who knew her said Sweets was one of those old witches who were mean for no reason. She was the type who would wish death on folks and spit in folks' food. That side of her Winter was just coming to know. If only she had kept her mouth closed.

Sweets was slim and trim. Even though she was sixty-two, she looked and functioned as if she was twenty years younger. She was the known cougar on the block, and she was proud of it. She would say, "Ain't nothing an old fool can do for me but give me his check, but if he wants my company he'll be waiting until he's dead. I like them young, good looking, and full of energy." Sweets was beautiful on the outside, but the woman had an evil soul. It was a shame how she had flipped on her own granddaughter to protect a dirty dog.

Sitting in the middle of the bed with her knees into her chest, tears spilled from a twelve-year-old Winter's eyes. To hear the woman who was supposed to love her scold her for sharing her painful secrets hurt her feelings. Sweets had no remorse for what the child had already suffered. Because Sweets hated Winter's mother, she hated her granddaughter, dismissing the fact that she was her so-called-favorite son's daughter. And the girl was his twin. Sweets, her deceased son, and Winter shared the same dark grey eyes, beautiful wavy, thick hair, and pointy nose. Winter's high cheekbones, thick lips, and mocha complexion she had inherited from her mother.

Winter's parents had been killed execution-style right in front of her. For hours, she had screamed her little lungs out until she was hoarse and drifted off to sleep. She did not rest well; the nightmares came back-to-back. Two days went by, and when Sweets had not heard from her son, she placed a call to the police station and requested a wellness check. That was when it was discovered the couple had been murdered. Winter was found lying between her deceased parents, asleep. Her clothes were smelly, and she looked pale and hardly kept her eyes open.

The officer who scooped the little girl in his arms almost broke down in tears, concluding the little girl would be forever scarred. He knew first-hand how a tragedy such as the one she had experienced could change a person forever— mentally and emotionally. It was going to take a lot of love, prayer, and therapy to help her heal. He prayed it worked out for her.

As Sweets pointed her long red acrylic nail at her granddaughter, the disdainful look on her face never wavered. "JUST LIKE YOUR LYING MAMA. SOMEBODY TRY TO HELP YOU, AND THIS IS THE THANKS THEY GET.

You lie!" she shrieked. "You're trying to destroy their life, but, baby, it's going to backfire on you just like it did your mama, that dirty, sleazy witch.

"I just wish my son had left that gold digger where he found her—right in the center of those nasty projects! You're next! You ain't going to live to see your twenty-first birthday. Watch and see what I tell you. God don't like ugly, and you're ugly for lying on your uncle like that!" Sweets rebuked.

Winter buried her knees further into her chest, and with her head down, she continued to shed tears. The thing was, she was not lying; her uncle had touched her. He had been touching her for quite some time now. She had finally gotten the courage to tell someone, as her dad had always coached her to do. He had said, "If anyone ever hurts you or touches you in your private areas, never be afraid to tell. Trust me, they won't get away with it. Don't ever think you did anything wrong." But her dad was dead and her mother was dead. All she had was her grandmother—whom she had thought she could confide in. Winter had believed Sweets would help her and protect her; instead, she had made her wish she'd never opened her mouth. That was a lesson she would never forget.

"You going to lie on the only son I have left? I should have left you in that foster home. I never should have picked you up. I know your mama's trifling ways got my son killed. Can't nobody tell me different. She was a snake out there on them drugs. A hooker..." Sweets shook her head. "Got my firstborn killed. They should have killed you when they killed her."

Sweets kind of felt bad about her last declaration toward her granddaughter, but she quickly shook it off. She wanted to knock some sense in the girl's head, but she knew if she hit her, she probably would have ended up killing her, and that was the reason she had to go. She only had one son left, and she refused to lose him because a little girl had evil ways like her mother.

"Sleep well tonight because tomorrow you're out of here. You're going to wish you hadn't lied, because them foster homes don't care about you. I tried!" she declared.

Not caring one bit that Winter was afraid of the dark, Sweets turned the light out, walked out the room, and slammed the room door behind her.

"No! Please turn the light back on. I am afraid of the dark, Sweets; please." Winter's cries fell on deaf ears. "Pleeease!"

Winter lay in bed, afraid of her past, her now, and what would happen to her next.

Her grandmother did not know her actions and cruel words would be the reason for Winter's screw-the-world mentality.

≈◆≋

It felt like, as soon as she drifted off to sleep, her grandmother was storming into the room. The sun was beaming through the thin curtains. Sweets' signature scent brought on that yucky feeling again. It was so heavy that Winter could taste it, and she felt sick to her stomach. Sweets snatched Winter by the arm, dragging her out the bed. Her body hit the floor, making a thumb sound.

"Ouch," Winter whimpered. It felt like her little hip was broken.

"Get up now and get dressed! Go take a bath too. When you are done, pack your stuff and come to me," she demanded. She never acknowledged the girl was in pain.

Winter sat one shopping bag, which held the few pieces of items she had come with, by the front door. She was too afraid to face her grandmother, scared of what she would say, and even more afraid of being sent away. Her uncle had hurt her a lot. He even had come in last night, and Sweets still didn't believe her.

In a fetal position, she lay in the bed crying and praying. The officer who'd picked up her had said, if she called on the angels, they would come, but all that ever came was nightmares and the evil person she called uncle.

The door squeaked. Winter didn't have to look; she knew it was him. Her first thought was to put up a fight and make as much noise as she could so Sweets would come. She balled her little fists up, and as soon as he sat on the bed and touched her leg, she began swinging.

"GET AWAY FROM ME! GET AWAY FROM ME!" she screamed and continued to swing.

"Ahhh! You hit me in the eye," he moaned.

Antwon used the back of his hand and knocked Winter in the face.

"Ohhhh!" she cried, holding her eye. It hurt so bad that it felt like he had knocked her left eye out of its socket, but she had to keep fighting. That was the only way her grandmother would believe her. She began to kick.

"STAY AWAY FROM ME!" she screamed and continued kicking.

"You sneaky little slut!" he growled.

Antwon jumped up and ran and turned the room light on. He quickly adjusted himself in his sweats. He cracked the room door, and Sweets entered moments later. With flared nostrils, her lip curled as she looked at Winter whimpering and holding her eye.

"Girl, shut up with all that!" he snarled.

She looked at her son, giving him the once-over. "I told you the lies she put on you. Why would you even come in here?" she asked, placing one hand on her hip.

"Because he wanna touch me. It's true," Winter sobbed.

"Stop lying! You're a whore just like your mama. You probably told him to come."

Sweets looked at her son. "Get out of this room! You stay away from her. Don't let her trick you no more."

"Yes, Mommy. I'm sorry," Antwon replied.

He gave Winter one last lustful look and left out the door. Sweets shut the light back out and slammed the room door. Winter lay there and cried.

"I'm going to kill him!" she muttered through her tears.

ᚣ◆ᚣ

Winter stood at the door with her head down, fiddling with the tip of her shirt.

"Get your ugly, big-lip self back in that room. No, I don't want you in there; go wait on the porch," Sweets ordered, pointing toward the front door.

With her head down, Winter opened the screen door and walked out, careful not to let the door slam.

It was one of the hottest days in August and the porch had no shade, so Winter was forced to sit in the hot sun. She sat on the hot step for what seemed like hours, and she became fatigued. She at least needed water, but she was too afraid to ask Sweets for anything. Her grandmother hated her and already wished she was dead. Just thinking about what she would say next frightened her.

A white Cadillac pulled up in front of the house, and Winter watched as an older black woman exited. It was Mrs. Nancy, the social worker. Winter smelled her and her stomach turned. Sweets came and stood at the door.

"Girl, I've been waiting for you to come get this snake," Sweet said to Ms. Nancy.

The woman was her old high school friend. She put you in the mind of Aunt Val from the *Fresh Prince of Bel Air*.

Ms. Nancy chuckled and fanned Sweets off as she climbed the four step up the porch. Stopping and looking at Winter, she scolded, "I don't know what you did to your grandmother, but whatever you did, you messed up." She shook her head.

"She sure did. Come on inside so I can tell you." Sweets ushered her inside.

"Can I have some water?" Winter asked, just above a whisper.

"Go drink from the water hose," Sweets snapped.

The women entered the house, and Sweets made sure to let the door slam behind her. Winter slowly walked down the stairs, heart rate slowing down. The heat had her feeling weak. She could not turn the water on fast enough. As she leaned over and drank from the water hose, tears ran down her face. Within a month, she had been through more than she could bear.

"Mommy! Daddy!" she cried. She could hear her grandma talking about her, and it made her cry even harder.

"Girl, she lied and said Antwon touched her. I caught her once before looking at music videos and shaking her skinny, stank behind in his face. I blame her mama, but still, she's gotta go. She tried to seduce her uncle," Sweets lied.

"Yeah. She came into my room one night too, asking me if I thought she was pretty. I told her I'd whoop her if she didn't leave my room. That hurt me, because that's my niece," Antwon chimed in.

"I'm so sorry," Ms. Nancy offered, covering her mouth with her right hand, her left on her chest. To learn Winter had made such dangerous accusations shocked her.

"It ain't your fault, Antwon; it's her mama's fault. She was raised by a whore," Sweets explained. "If she does not get help, she is going to grow up just like her."

"Well, she'll regret it; now no one will want to adopt her. She messed up. Let me go get her placed somewhere, because I don't even wanna be around her," the social worker stated. "I can't stand a liar, and to lie about something like that, she'd better be glad I cannot put my hands on her."

Winter cried. Her heart ached. No one believed her. She began to get nervous, wondering where she would go from there. Would more men touch her? The thought, paired with the heat, caused Winter to become exhausted, and she fainted on the grass.

Chapter Two:
A COUPLE OF YEARS LATER — A LIFE OF SIN

"Wake up."

Winter looked up at her foster sister/friend. It was Asia. She was tall and thick with big breasts, wide hips, and a big apple bottom. She looked like she was in her twenties, but was only fifteen.

"What? " Winter complained.

"Girl, wake up. It's time. We about to get this-nigga and pay him back for what he did to us!" Asia asserted.

She was hyped. She was tired of being hurt and no one doing anything about it, so now she was going to have her own back and handle it how she saw fit.

The declaration was a trigger for Winter, and the trauma she had suffered from her uncle came back to her remembrance. Winter rose straight up in the bed. She glanced to her right at the small digital clock on the nightstand. It was almost midnight.

"Is Janice asleep?" Winter asked, referring to her fifth caregiver since she had left Sweets. This particular house she had been placed in was in the projects where she had lived with her parents. Although it brought back bad memories, it felt like home, and Janice was nowhere near as bad as the others. All she did was drink and host card games, and as long as the girls did their schoolwork and chores, she did not trip on them.

"Yeah, she's asleep. Now, go get ready. If we take too long, Tink is going to leave. I can tell she don't really wanna go. Go, get dressed, Sis."

Winter gave her foster sister a head nod and jumped up from the bed. She crossed over the small room and grabbed her jeans and hoodie she had placed on the folding chair before she went to sleep.

Dressed in all black, the two teens jumped from the second floor and made their way on foot to 1615 Belhaven Street, where they met up with their friend Tink.

"I don't think I wanna do this," Tink said, tapping her hand on the steering wheel.

Tink resembled Strawberry Shortcake and her name fit her perfectly. She was four-four, with cinnamon complexion, sandy brown hair, and freckles on her nose.

"Man, we're here now, and it was your idea," Winter reminded her.

It was true. When Winter and Asia shared with her what had happened to them at the hands of a grown man, she got angry and wanted revenge for her friends.

Secretly, she wanted revenge for her mom too. Her mother had been kidnapped by her neighbor when she was thirteen. He had taken her to Vegas and pimped her for almost two months before she was found. In her eyes, her father had gotten away free. They had sent him back to Mexico, leaving her mother with a child she had not asked for but loved deeply. Her mother had not gotten justice, but she would for her and her friends tonight.

"Hop in; let's go," Tink said, just above a whisper.

Winter climbed in the backset and Asia in the front.

Tink started her mom's car and headed across town to the projects, not too far from where they stayed.

Winter thought, '*Finally I get to show this-nigga how it feels to be the weakest link.*'

The ride was silent. Each girl was occupied with her own thoughts. When they approached the corner of the projects, Asia said, "It's him or us. We ain't leaving nothing behind!"

"I think we should park right here. That way, no one will see my mom's car," Tink suggested.

"Cool," Asia replied.

"Let's go!" Winter ordered, and they filed out the whip.

'*The dough and his life—I want it all,*' Winter thought.

They were three teenagers whose mission was to do what the system and other adults had failed to do—protect.

When they left, the girls were so juiced. They now had a come-up. He had loot and drugs, and they took it all. Unknown to the others, Winter had caught her first body. Her uncle was dead, and she hoped, when her grandmother found out, she would die too. Now she could move on.

YEARS LATER....

Chapter Three:
LOYALTY OVER EVERYTHING

Winter is in a deep sleep from the early morning events in the field. She has come up on the bag, and now her savings account is up by a substantial amount. She had gone on a solo mission: She followed a couple home she met in the bar and robbed them of their Rolex watches and wedding rings. After successfully hitting her lick, she went to the house, took a hot shower, and relaxed for a few hours. Then she hit up her connect to get rid of the merchandise.

When she is done, she calls her dude to let him know she wants to hook up. The pair enjoy a meal at his favorite spot on the strip, do a little shopping, and later return to her pad. Her boo gives it to her until she is in a coma. He showers, changes his clothes, and dips to hang out with his boys at the golf course.

BOOM-BOOM-BOOM!

Winter's eyes pop open. She wasn't intending to wake up until the next day, but the constant banging on her front door and the ringing of her doorbell screw up her peaceful slumber.

"What?!" she roars.

Sitting straight up in her king-size bed, she squints her eyes due to the bright light. She still is afraid of the dark. The only time she sleeps with the lights out is when her man stays with her, but even then, she has a tiny light in the outlet closest to her bed. Winter reaches for her gun on the nightstand. Squeezing her eyes shut in an attempt to adjust them to the light, it takes a minute for her pupils to adjust. That doesn't stop her from grabbing her gun and hopping off the bed, ready to blaze if she has to.

"Who is it?!" she growls as she stomps from her bedroom to the living room.

Winter knows it isn't the police, as they would have bypassed the formalities and kicked the door in. Not many people know where she lays her head. One, she doesn't mess with many people, and two, those she allows in her space know she doesn't play about popping up at her pad. Being from the streets and the victim of a couple of tragedies in her young life have caused paranoia and trust issues, and she doesn't put anything past anyone. The life she lives is either them or her, and she isn't ready to go. That is why her Glock is kept loaded and cocked.

With caution, she aims toward her front door, stepping to the side just in case they fire first.

"WHO IS IT?!" Winter yells.

"It's meeee—Summer!" she cries.

Hearing her sweet friend crying, Winter becomes alarmed.

'What's the matter? What could have happened?' she thinks.

She lowers her gun and darts to the door, her hands shaking as she undoes the top and bottom locks. Snatching the door open, Winter freezes. All the wind from her lungs vanishes. She can hardly catch her breath. She takes a step back, closes her eyes and reopens them, hoping she is dreaming.

Winter cannot believe what she was seeing. There her friend stands with bruises all over her beautiful face. Her hair is disheveled and her T-shirt ripped. Someone has hurt her, and Winter is pissed. Summer is shivering like a leaf on a tree. Her friend doesn't even have shoes on and is standing there with two shopping bags in her hand with her clothes spilling out.

"What happened to you?" Winter pulls her by her arm into the house, shuts her front door, and locks it back.

Summer stands there, trembling.

"What happened to you?" Winter repeats.

"Aunt Vee and Kelly jumped on me," Summer manages to say through her tears. She is heartbroken.

Winter has to take an extra step back, and she chuckles to keep from exploding. She is ready to bust her gun on Summer's folks and whoever is rolling with them. Like her, Summer has already been through it. She isn't with all the action like Winter is. That is one of the reasons she is so angry. Summer doesn't bother with anyone. She is drama-free.

"Summer, go shower and lie in my bed. The sheets are clean." She offers a smile.

"K," Summer replies. She puts her head down and limps toward the bedroom.

"Ba-beeee, y'all done messed up now!" Vee and her daughter are about to feel the wrath of Winter Santiago.

Summer is her girl. Her boo. Her heart. She is someone she wishes she could be—innocent, sweet, goal-driven—but it is too late for that. Winter was born to a savage, and she is one herself, All she can do is live through Summer and protect her at all costs. If it wasn't for Summer, Winter would probably be in jail for murder. She is the only one who can calm her down and talk her out of most things that could cost her life.

Winter is very overprotective of the people she considers family. Besides her man, Summer is all she holds close. Tink is Winter's homegirl, but for some reason, she has not allowed her to get as close as she has Summer. Tink is like her—get it by any means necessary—whereas Summer is a good girl.

Winter and Summer have been in each other's lives since they were fourteen. Unlike her and Tink, Summer and Winter do not hang together often, but Summer is still her favorite. She and Summer live two different lifestyles. Winter is deemed a savage by the streets, and depending on who you ask, she will die a failure. Summer is the good girl, the cute nerd, who is going to be someone in life.

Winter was already in the system when Summer came to her foster home. Unlike the other kids, Winter didn't pay any attention to who came or went; all she had was herself, so that was all she worried about. One day, she decided to go into the backyard to get some fresh air. Taking a seat on the porch, she watched as two of the house bullies got all up in the new girl's face. She couldn't hear what they were saying because she had her earphones on. She watched as the girl was shoved to the ground, and one bully pulled her hair. The stud lifted her dress and started laughing as she pointed at her private parts.

That act triggered Winter. She jumped up from the porch, charged over to the trio, and commenced to whooping on the stud girl. Her friend didn't even bother to jump in. Everyone knew Winter didn't mind fighting, and if she couldn't whoop you, she wouldn't give up until she got revenge. In another home, Winter had poured bleach all over one boy and tried to set him on fire. The girl was bad.

"Don't you ever in your life come near her again! You are nasty, and I *hate* nasty people!" Winter growled. "I will kill you!" she warned, scaring the chick even more.

From that day forward, Winter took a liking to Summer. She didn't know why, because no way was she friendly. Although they were the same age, Winter considered Summer as her little homegirl and kept her close by. Winter had a hustle, and she made sure when she brought herself anything, she got Summer something too. In her opinion, Summer deserved it.

One year later, Summer's aunt was granted custody of her. The duo had promised to stay in touch but had lost contact. Winter didn't know that Summer had preferred it that way. Summer wanted to disconnect from anything and anyone in the foster home she considered a prison she had lived in. She believed they all deserved each other, and Winter was a villain just like them.

Winter and Summer reconnected seven months ago when Summer serviced her in the McDonald's drive-thru. Winter feels like she is doing well, considering all she has been through. She shared with Summer how she is content with her life. She has her own place, a car, a man who is fine and adores her, and her pockets stay laced. Her current life is better than it has ever been. She shared with Summer a few secrets. Summer told her she is better than she thinks she is and her mistakes don't define her.

Summer, on the other hand, had been living in hell ever since she left the group home. Unfortunately, it has not gotten better for her. The stories she shared about her so-called aunt and cousin are sad. Only a foolish person wouldn't know Summer's family isn't worth two dead rats, and they are very much envious of her. Her cousin is a big yellow ape with spots all over her face. Thirty years old and messing with a broke-and-busted twenty year old who still lives with his momma and using public transportation. Her aunt is just as pitiful. All she does is mess with men in jail who only use her when they are locked up.

'They didn't have to do her like that!' Winter flops down on the sofa. *'They are going to have to see me!'* Winter swears, meaning every word.

ॐ ♦ ॐ

"I just don't understand why they did me like this. I would never betray my family. I would never betray them."

Tears spill from Summer's eyes as she sits in the passenger seat of Winter's hot-pink Impala, thinking about the drama that went down. Tupac's *Thug Mansion* blares from the speakers. The windows are down, allowing a nice breeze to keep them cool. Winter bobs her head to the music as she envisions how she is going to knock the heads off those who hurt her friend.

Summer sits silently, and her tears won't stop falling. She wishes she could lie under the covers and sleep the days away until she is over what happened to her. But Winter will not allow such a thing; she resolves everything with violence. A small part of her cares about Winter, but she does not like the other side of her—the side does wicked things for money and hurts people she believes deserve it.

Summer will never admit her true feelings: one, she is scared of Winter, and two, Winter is the only one who helps her with money when she needs it. She keeps her on reserve for hard times, but other than that, she avoids her as much as she can.

Winter parks on the next street over from where they are going. She cuts the car off and looks at Summer's bruised-up face. A fire is still burning inside her.

"Let's go!" Winter demands.

"Why did you park over here?" Summer asks.

Winter looks dead in her eyes. "I was going to have you wait here while I shot the house up, but I changed my mind. I think you will get better satisfaction with me beating them until they wish they were dead," she bluntly states.

Summer's eyes widen from fear. After two attempts, she is able to swallow the brick in her throat. *'God, I wish I had another friend. This girl is sick!' Summer thinks.*

"Are you going to get out or not?" Winter questions.

Summer's eyes pop open. She attempts to speak, but Winter speaks first.

"How long are you going to be a pushover? They do not care about you. Those people have been dogging you from day one; you said it. Summer, if you don't get out of this car and show them you are not to be played with..." Winter warns. She doesn't even have to finish her threat.

Summer nods her head in agreement. "You're right," she says, just above a whisper.

As the duo stroll up the block, Summer can feel her heart beating in her chest. Her hands are clammy and she is nervous as heck. Her thoughts go back to what Winter said. She is right: Her aunt and cousin have hated her from the day they took her from foster care and had no shame in letting her know. But the physical and emotional abuse just isn't enough to make her not want them in her life. They are her dad's family, and she loved her dad and she knew her dad had loved them.

Winter stops in mid-stride. She and Summer make eye contact. "If they jump me, you'd better jump in."

Winter has never thought about putting hands on Summer, but if she leaves her hanging, she is going to at least smack her. When the pair approach the house, one of the culprits is sitting on the porch. Summer slows her pace, but Winter wastes no time walking into the yard. She goes for the biggest and loudest—the aunt. Vee jumps up from the chair she is sitting in.

"What is your big-lip, black, ugly dog-looking-ass going to do?"

With a closed fist, Winter draws back and punches Vee dead in her kisser. All she feels are teeth across her knuckles.

Summer watches as Winter punches her aunt so hard that she flies back on the chair and it tilts backward. Winter dives on top of Vee with a closed fist and begins hammering her in the face.

Kelly runs out the house, yelling and screaming, "YOU GOT ME TWISTED, TRAMP! GET UP OFF MY MOMMA!" She jumps on Winter's back and begins punching her in the head.

Summer does not want any part of what is going on, but she has no choice. Her family has disowned her, and Winter is all she has. She bolts into the yard, snatches her cousin by the hair, and slams her to the ground. All the hurt and built-up frustration are released on one of the people who caused her trauma.

"I HATE YOU! I HATE ALL OF YOU! YOU ARE LOSERS! YOU WILL NEVER BE ANYTHING! YOU HATE ME BECAUSE I AM NOT GHETTO TRASH!" Summer screams as she punches and curses. "EVERYONE IS JEALOUS OF ME BECAUSE I'M SMART AND PRETTY! I'M TIRED OF Y'ALL!"

Winter has already laid out Vee, and when she turns around to see the damage Summer is doing to Kelly, she is shocked. She had no idea her girl had hands.

"Come on; let's go. You got her; let's go," Winter says as she grabs Summer off her bloody cousin, but Summer keeps punching her. Winter can't make out what she is saying, but she isn't herself.

Pow!

The gunshot shakes Summer from her stupor. Winter has pulled her own gun out, but when she sees it is a neighbor firing in the air, she puts her gun away.

"Ahhh!" Summer squeals. She looks on in horror as her cousin lies on the ground with blood all over her face. She cannot believe what she has done.

"Let's go." Winter pulls her by the arm.

Police cars can be heard in the distance.

"We've got to go! I ain't trying to go to jail!"

Summer's eyes land on her aunt and her mouth drops. She isn't moving. "Is she dead? Oh my god!"

"I said, let's go!" Winter yanks her so hard she almost falls. As Winter pulls her down the street, Summer cries all the way.

"GIRL, GET IN THE CAR OR GET LEFT!" Winter bellows. She is tired of her dramatics.

ର ◆ ঙ

'Summer! You will not have a panic attack! Why did you allow Winter to talk you into doing that?' she thinks.

Summer looks at Winter, who is steering the car with one hand and bobbing her head to the music, unbothered.

'One day, you are going to get what's coming to you!' Summer curses her only friend.

Days after what went down, Summer can't sleep, haunted by her childhood. The suffering of panic attacks and unwanted thoughts of being just like her mother are driving her crazy.

Summer is standing in the middle of the guest bedroom floor at Winter's house, humming as loud as she can, trying to drown out the lies she is hearing in her head:

'You are evil.'

'You are crazy like your mama.'

'You are going to prison.'

'Your mama gotta away, but you won't.'

She puts her hands over her ears and continues to hum. When she has calmed down a little bit, Summer runs and grabs her cellphone from her purse on the bed. She dials her aunt's number; after not getting an answer the second time, she dials Kelly. She hopes they aren't badly hurt—or worse, dead. She begins to pace the room, biting her nonexistent nails as she waits for the call to connect. Summer stops in the mirror and stares into her eyes.

'I am not her.'

"Hello; you know what to do." ***Beep!***

"Kelly, I'm sorry; I didn't mean it. Winter forced me. I just wanted to leave it alone. Tell Auntie I'm not like my mom. I don't hurt people. I love my family. I am so sorry. She threw away all my medications, and you know what happens when I don't take them. Please call me."

She hangs up. The fear of being a killer is taking a toll on her mind. The only thing that will calm her down completely is the meds she doesn't enjoy taking, but she needs them. Summer goes into the closet, grabs the Mickey Mouse backpack, and pulls out a white plastic bag containing several pill bottles. She pops the top on each and pours the pills in her hand. She tosses the three pills in her mouth and begins to chew. She frowns and almost gags from the taste, but she needs the pills to work fast. She is about to go crazy. Summer then places the pills back in the bag and again hides the bag in the back of the closet in the hamper. She slides down on the floor, going into a trance. Her scattered brain takes her back to her childhood.

"Lala-lala-lala…"

She watches as the young girl skips toward the house and onto the porch.

"I am warning you. I'm watching you. You will not leave. I mean it!" Her mom's voice roars like a lion's.

At eight years old, Summer is accustomed to what her dad calls, "Mommy having a temper tantrum." Summer stops at the steps, takes a seat on the porch, and begins to sing as loud as she can to drown out the noise. Before she knows it, the sun is down and the commotion has ceased. Summer grabs the flowers she has picked for her mom and the stones she found for her dad. She plans on giving them to them at the dinner table.

"Mommy, Daddy," she calls as she walks through the house. The living room is empty. She glances at the kitchen, noticing there is nothing on the stove. Her stomach growls, she is hungry. Summer walks down the hall into her bedroom.

"AHHHHHHHH!" she shrieks.

She freezes. All she can do is scream as she stares at her dad sprawled out on her bedroom floor. Blood covers his upper body. Her heart drops and her mouth falls agape upon seeing a knife in his chest. She hears a chuckle and slowly turns her head to the left. Her mom is sitting on the floor next to her dad.

"Mommy! What happened to Daddy?" Summer mumbles.

"He wanted to leave us, Summer," her mother answers as she lights a cigarette. "He wanted to leave us because I'm crazy."

Her mother breaks out into thunderous laughter as she looks at her daughter and puts the cigarette to her lips. Summer watches as she pulls on the cigarette and blows out the smoke through her nose.

"I am not crazy; he's the one who's crazy. How dare he think he could leave me!" She bellows.

Summer slowly pedals backward. Her mother leaps up from the floor, gawking at her young daughter as she snatches the knife from her husband's chest.

"HE IS THE ONE WHO'S CRAZY! HOW DARE HE THINK HE WAS GOING TO LEAVE ME TO BE A SINGLE MOTHER! I DIDN'T WANT YOU; HE DID!"

Summer continues to back up; for the first time, she is afraid of her mother.

"Oh, you scared? Well, how about I send you with your dad." She cackles.

She charges at Summer, but she takes off running... speeding through the house like a road runner.

She escaped her mother's wrath. However, she can't run from the sins of her mother.

ॐ ♦ ॐ

'You will never be happy. Never! You know why? Because you were bonded by sin. Bad luck will always find you. You will never be stable. You have your mother's blood.She cursed you and if you ever have kids they will be cursed too. You'll never be free.'

It is the voice. She placed her hands over her ears. Summer springs up from the floor. The voice she hasn't heard since she was a teenager is back. That is the voice that made her cut herself. Cutting was her way of trying to get rid of her mother's DNA.

'These pills have to hurry and kick in.'

Summer rocks back and forth until she is relaxed and falls asleep.

Chapter Four:
ANOTHER DAY

Contemporary R&B fills the establishment as the patrons enjoy one of the hottest restaurants at L.A. Live.

"So, did you ever find out why they jumped on her and put her out?" Tink asks.

She and Winter are sitting across from each other at Shaquille O'Neal's restaurant. Winter normally doesn't tell her friends' business, but she is in her feelings. Since the fight, Summer barely has said two words to her. All Summer does is go to school, to work, and to her room. At first, she thought the girl was just depressed due to the lies her aunt tried to put on her, but now Summer's vibes are coming off as if she is mad at her. All she did was have her back.

"They claimed she was messing with the aunt's dude, but we know that is a lie." Winter pops a fry in her mouth.

"And how do we know that?" Tink asks, looking at Winter.

"You know she doesn't want him."

Tink purses her lips and bats her eyes. "Well, he is cute, and has a body and money. We don't know what happened. But let me shut up, because we know you think the girl is an angel."

"What beef do you have with her?" Winter inquires with a disdainful look on her face.

"Excuse you? First off, I don't think or care enough about the girl to have beef. Like I said before, she doesn't seem so innocent to me, and that is how I feel. But even then, I didn't have beef. Now, I have beef because she is living at your house, acting funny with you, and you are the one who protected her. Your freedom is on the line." Tink rolls her eyes, sits back in her seat, and crosses her arms. "I don't trust her. If them people press charges, she will blame you."

"Gon with that! This is street politics; no one's pressing charges. And Summer would never!"

"Oh, okay. Well, if she ever betrays you, I am going to light her up and repent later!"

She is dead serious. She genuinely cares for Winter. Winter has her flaws like everyone else, but she is a good person. Even her mom thinks so, and she doesn't fool with anyone Tink hangs with.

Winter ignores Tink's comment about what she will do to Summer. She is all talk; she knows better.

"Tomorrow is friends and family day. Are you going to come to church with me?" Tink asks.

She leans forward, grabs her water, and takes a sip, then sits back as she looks at Winter, waiting for a response.

Winter shakes her head, no. Tink already knew she would decline; she has for the last three months. However, she will not stop asking her.

"So, you're really into the church stuff, huh?" Winter asks.

She picks up a fry, then tosses it back on her plate. She isn't feeling well. Her mouth begins to water.

Before Tink can reply, Winter jumps up and runs through the restaurant toward the restroom. Tink runs after her.

BOOM! PLOP!

Winter runs smack into a hard chest and falls on her butt.

"Dang!" Tink complains, looking at the person who made her friend fall.

From the floor, Winter looks up into the eyes of a handsome chocolate man. Her man is fine, but the chocolate god before her looks as if he was handcrafted by her herself. Every visible feature is pulling Winter more and more into him. His skin is smooth and seems so tasty. His thick, bushy eyebrows are set above beautiful, oval-shaped, walnut-colored eyes. His eyelashes are just as thick and long as hers. Even his soup-coolers are attractive. Winter hates her own big lips but thinks his are perfect.

Tink is standing behind her with her mouth open, gazing at the same fine specimen of a man.

Bazz is tall, dark, and toned. His half-smile displays pearly-white teeth and a dimple so deep it makes her seasick. Being alert to everything going on around him, Bazz peeps how both of the women are in awe of him. He is used to it; he is *that* dude. The women want him, and the dudes love to hate him, but at the same time want to be him. He is used to the attention, but it still boosts his ego when pretty girls lust over him. Bazz looks down at Winter and extends his hand.

"I apologize," Bazz says. '*She's fine. Mean-looking, but fine,*' he thinks.

Winter being Winter refuses his help. She jumps up off the floor and runs into the restroom, throwing up all over the floor before she makes it to the stall.

"You are too fine. Stay right here; I need your number," Tink says before rushing off to check on her friend.

Bazz chuckles. He wouldn't mind getting old girl's numbers with the juicy lips, but he has things to do. He is sure he will see her around.

"FRIIIEEENND... ARE YOU PREGNANT?" Tink yells.

She is so loud everyone up and down the hallway can hear her. That is Bazz' cue to get on. Little mama has a situation he wants no part of.

❧ ✦ ❧

Him: *I LOVE YOU.*

Winter rests her head against her car window, staring into a daze. She isn't ready to go home. The throwing up scared her because it confirms what she has suspected ever since she missed her period.

'I can't have a baby,' she thinks.

Winter: *LOVE YOU TOO.*, she finally texts back.

Him: *YOU FEEL LIKE GETTING PRETTY? I WILL SCOOP YOU AFTER I LEAVE THIS MEETING AND WE CAN GO TO DINNER, THEN CHILL AT THE LOUNGE.*

Winter: *NAH. GO AHEAD. I AM GOING TO REST, PLUS MY SHOW COMES ON TONIGHT. LOL*

When Noah doesn't text back, she knows he is feeling some kind of way. If it were up to him, he would be under her every day, but Winter doesn't want that even though she loves her guy. She has never imagined herself with a wholesome man like Noah. She doesn't know what he sees in her, but what she does know is what they have will not last. They are from two different walks of life.

Winter: *GOOD NIGHT LOVE BUG.*

Chapter Five:
LATER THAT DAY

In her short-shorts and half-top, Summer stands over the stove, singing as she stirs the pepper steak she is cooking. Summer is in the best mood she has been in all week. The pills coupled with the stress relief was needed, but she promised herself that was the first and last time she would allow her aunt's man to come near her. Thoughts of the night her aunt and cousin jumped her resurface.

⦲◆⦳

"You are sneaky, messing with my man!"

POP!

Vee slaps her niece so hard in her sleep that Summer screams and sits up in the bed. For a moment, she is confused. Her eyes are narrowed in on her aunt. Vee is holding her cellphone in her hand, pointing it at her.

"You can't lie either; here is the proof," she snarls, holding the phone up.

Summer tries to explain, but her aunt starts punching her. All she can do is ball up in a knot and take the beating.

"I'm sorry. I'm sorry. It was just a text," she whimpers.

Vee punches and curses her for a good while. She hears her cousin's voice calling her names.

"Dirty, nasty slut, sleeping with your aunt's man. I don't play about my momma."

She is snatched by her hair, and her body hits the floor like a sack of potatoes. Pain shoots through her entire body as she is punched repeatedly.

"I'm a virgin. I never slept with him. It was a text; it didn't mean anything," Summer whimpers.

"YOU GOT TWO SECONDS TO GET AWAY FROM MY HOUSE, OR YOU WILL WISH YOU WERE DEAD. YOU TRIED THE WRONG ONE!" her aunt yells. "YOU AIN'T GOING TO HAVE NO GOOD LUCK, BECAUSE YOU'RE FOUL."

As she recalls that night's events, she has mixed emotions about how her family handled her. The text between her and her aunt's man was wrong, but he had flirted with her for months before she flirted back. She had not planned on doing anything with her aunt's man. She just liked the attention, but why hadn't she confronted him? She is family, not him.

'*Since you blamed me, now I did it. That was only to pay you back for choosing him over your blood,*' she thinks as she adds more seasoning to the meat.

That morning, her aunt's dude had texted, asking if she was okay. She had replied, asking him how her aunt and cousin were doing. Vee has just gotten out of the hospital from a concussion, and Kelly is fine. He then offered her money to help her get by since it was his fault she was kicked out. Summer met up with him at his cousin's place. They talked, she got the money, and she allowed him to explore her body with his mouth. It was her second experience with a man, and she can honestly say she enjoyed it, but she is done with him.

The tap on Summer's shoulder causes her to jump in fear. She turns around and comes face-to-face with a handsome guy. She takes the earphones off her ears and smiles.

"Noah, you scared me." She laughs nervously.

"My bad. I was calling your name." Noah looks over at the food on the stove. "Smells good and it's my favorite," he admits.

She grins. "Cool. Do you know when Winter is coming? We can all eat together."

"I didn't tell her I was coming. She will be here in a minute. Her show comes on tonight." He looks back at the stove. "I could get used to home-cooked meals. I know Winter appreciates you." Winter can't cook.

"I haven't been cooking lately, I wasn't feeling well, but I will now," she assures him.

"Cool. Let me go take a shower and pick up her room so she can relax. I know she's got clothes all over the place." He chuckles before leaving.

Summer watches him until he is no longer in view. Until this day, she cannot understand what a nice guy like him is doing with a savage like Winter. He is one of those pretty boys. In her opinion, the couple is not a match. Taking a deep breath, she shakes the thoughts she has of Winter's man and finishes cooking. She then sets the table.

'*I wonder if he can make me feel like Aunt Vee's man does.*' She giggles at her devious thoughts. '*Summer, stop it!*'

Chapter Six:
FEAR

Winter isn't scared of anyone. All her life she has had to defend herself. She has fought, stabbed up a couple of chicks, and even murdered. She doesn't let anyone put her down, but this time, she clammed up. His stare alone felt like bullets to her heart.

"Understand this..." Mr. McGuire looked her up and down. "You are nothing but a piece-of-ass. You're his little experiment, nothing more. Don't get comfortable, because I will protect mine at all costs!" he had warned.

Whenever she thinks about opening up to her man, his father's words comes as a reminder of who she can never be. At times, she believes it is true. Her grandmother was the first person to plant the seeds that she is nothing and will never be anything, and that she is a curse like her mother. Others came behind her and watered the seeds her granny had planted. Whether she wants to accept it or not, her insecurities are heightened each time she is belittled.

When guys says she is pretty, she assumes it is only because of her grey eyes. When people like Tink's mom and Noah speak highly of her, it is hard for her to believe they are real. She just doesn't see it. In her opinion, she isn't smart like Summer and nowhere near as pretty as she is. Tink is pretty and smart too. Unlike her, Tink doesn't have to do what they are doing for money. She has a good support system and even has her nursing degree.

Winter, on the other hand, has no one because they have abandoned her and never cared about her in the first place. She doesn't even know what she wants out of life. Deep down, she feels worthless. The material things she has acquired mean nothing when her spirit is broken. It means nothing when she is secretly drowning and too cowardly to die. What she has means nothing when she is *covered in sin*. She prays she isn't pregnant. She doesn't know if she will be able to live with herself after killing a baby—because for sure, she can never be a mom. The baby will be cursed, just as she is.

Winter's phone vibrates. She has a feeling it is Noah. She saw his car in the guest parking when she pulled up. She grabs her things, preparing to get out the car. Looking down at her cellphone, she sees the text is from Tink.

Tink: **I CAN DO ALL THINGS THROUGH CHRIST JESUS WHO STRENGTHENS ME. SAY THAT WHENEVER YOU FEEL CONFUSED OR UNSURE. WEAK. TIRED. TRY IT.**

Winter: **OK.**

Winter isn't into all that God-stuff, but the way she is feeling, she will give anything a try. She doesn't know how much longer she can hold on. She is drowning and no one can see it, so they cannot help, and even when they try, she refuses to share her fears. Showing vulnerability is a sign of weakness, and predators will waste no time eating her up and spitting her out. So, she carries everything in a vault that only she can access.

Winter walks into the house and her stomach begins to growl; the food smells delicious. She loves Summer's cooking and she is starving, but she cannot risk eating and throwing up again, especially not in front of Noah.

Winter closes the front door, drops her keys on the end table, then makes her way to the kitchen. Summer is over the stove, so she doesn't see Winter when she entered. Winter gives her the once-over, peeping how she has on her red Pretty girl lounge set. She goes into the fridge and grabs a bottle of water. When she turns around, Summer is staring at her.

"What's up?" Winter tosses her head.

"I cooked. I was hoping we could all eat together."

"I ain't hungry, but it smells good."

"Aww, okay. Well, tell Noah the food is ready. I am going to go to my room. Thanks for letting me stay."

"No problem. Do you mind making Noah's plate? I do not feel well. I'm tired and just want to shower. He acts like a baby, and he needs his plate fixed." Winter smiles.

"Sure."

"Thanks."

Winter leaves the kitchen. When she walks into her room, she smiles at her man asleep in the recliner. When he hears her enter, his eyes open. Noah stands up and walks over to his woman. Pulling her into his arms, he buries his face in her neck. Noah is so in-tune with Winter, that when her heart is heavy, he can feel it. Winter is the type who will snap and shut down if she feels she is being pressured into being vulnerable, so he has learned to refrain from asking her about her feelings.

કે ✦ ➷

Winter and Noah met in their last year in high school. Winter was new to the school, and based on her disposition alone, she was deemed a tough girl whom no one dared try to be friends with. It didn't bother her; she wasn't friendly anyway. Her unique features made her attractive to most. It was the juicy lips, high cheekbones, dark grey eyes, and tattooed arms that drew most toward her, including Noah.

Noah McGuire. He was popular just by being handsome, funny, charming, and laid back. Noah came from a family of wealth. On top of that, he was fine: light skin, tight eyes, full lips, with thick, curly jet-black hair. Noah was biracial. His father was half-Black and white. His mother was full-blown Asian; it was from her that he got his height. Noah was five-eight but had the heart of a lion. His cockiness and boldness was how he had gotten his gangsta girl. She was the only chick he had had to fight to get her attention, the only girl who had shut him down more than a dozen times.

Since she refused to give him her number, he had had to get it the illegal way. He'd had one of his groupies steal it from the office, along with her address. Since she wouldn't give him any play at school, he had pulled up to her house one Saturday afternoon and was taken by surprise at what he witnessed.

Winter was standing in the middle of the yard, surrounded by what looked to be her clothes. A short, heavyset Black woman was yelling at her, and a short, stocky white boy around their age was standing there like he was waiting for something to pop off.

Noah threw his car into park and jumped out.

"What's up, Winter? You good?" Noah asked, walking up like he was with all the business, and he was. When a hater tried to come at him on some rah-rah type of drama, they quickly found out that the short-in-

height pretty boy had hands. Not only was he a black belt, but he knew how to box too. Noah held his own.

Winter's eyes sparked. She couldn't believe Noah was there. He had been flirting with her since she'd stepped in his school. She thought he was cute, but she'd refused to give him the time of the day. There were dozens of girls who were more his type and speed. Her life was too dark for him—plus, she wasn't on his level—but his flirting was causing her to secretly wish she could date someone like Noah. His pulling up on her had her on cloud nine. She couldn't believe he was actually at her house.

"What are you doing here?" she asked, trying her best to hide her smile.

"I came to see you, and I am glad I did. Is this your stuff out here?" His eyes surveyed the area.

"Yeah, I'm good," she assured him.

"Who-in-the-hell are you?!" the woman asked.

"I'm her MAN. Why do y'all got her out here like this?" he asked, mean-mugging the woman.

Winter stood there with wide eyes and butterflies in her tummy. One of the most popular boys at school was claiming her.

"None of your business. You don't question my mom," the guy said, walking toward Noah.

"If I were you, I would pipe it down. Pick up her clothes and apologize for disrespecting her," he warned.

The pair whom had just tossed Winter out were her foster mom and her son. They had accused Winter of stealing and were threatening to make her life miserable if she did not give the money back.

"She'd better give that money back!" the boy advised.

"I ain't got your money, and you cannot make me leave; you get paid for me to be here!" Winter countered.

The woman ran up to Winter and went to hit her, but Winter ducked the punch and gave the lady a two-piece that sent her on her behind. Noah didn't even give the son time to do anything. He hit him with one punch and a hard kick to the gut, putting him on his back.

"I JUST CALLED THE COPS; YOU ARE GOING DOWN!" the sister yelled from the upstairs window.

Winter looked at Noah. She didn't want to get him in any drama.

"Get out of here. I got it."

"Nah, I ain't leaving without you," he rebutted, staring directly into her grey eyes.

It was the sincerity in his voice, the look in his eyes, and how he stood there, not caring about the consequences, that had her in awe of him. Her heart smiled and cried at the same time. It had been years since she had felt as if a man cared about her, and that man was her dad.

"Come on, Winter, let's go. You can leave those clothes. It ain't nothing to get you some more gear."

Dazed, Winter batted her eyes at him. Without responding, she walked over and began collecting her clothes and shoes off the ground. She wanted to go inside and get her other things, but her gut told her to just leave them and go.

Winter left with Noah and had him take her to a motel. She had money saved from her hustle, plus the two grand she had taken from the group home. She wasn't worried. She had a plan. She was three months shy of eighteen, so she knew the cops weren't going to look for her. As far as the money was concerned, they had to prove she had it.

Winter stayed away from school, but on the third day, Noah popped up to the motel with her schoolwork and a home-cooked meal. From that day forward, the two were a couple. Noah caught a lot of criticism from his friends, coaches, and girls about Winter and her background, but he didn't care. Her flawed life made him desire her that much more.

"She will bring you down. She has nothing to lose, but you have everything to lose," his father warned.

Noah was like his mother; he did not live based on others' opinions. Winter loved him for who he was and not what he had. She hardly ever took anything from him unless it was a holiday or her birthday. When Noah elected to attend USC instead of Harvard, his dad flipped out, but his mom understood. Noah didn't care what anyone said, Winter was his girl. He just wished she would open up more and trust him with her heart.

Although she wants to stay in his arms all night, Winter is the first one to pull away. She looks into her man's eyes, the two share a long, passionate kiss, and Winter pulls away again.

"Summer made your plate for me; go eat. I'm going to take a shower," she tells him with a half-grin.

"You aren't eating?" he asks.

"I'm not hungry, just tired. I wanna sleep," she answers, barely able to look him in the eyes.

He gives her a head nod, feeling jaded that she has shut him down, but he won't address it. He heads to the door and stops, turns and looks at Winter, who is digging in her drawer.

"After almost two years, you still can't tell me what's on your mind." Noah shakes his head and leaves the room. He is trying his best with Winter, but he is getting tired of trying to make her receive his love without boundaries.

Winter takes a deep breath and lets it out. She cares for Noah, but she knows it is only a matter of time before he leaves her.

"Hey, I made your plate," Summer says excitedly when Noah walks into the kitchen. "I was just about to bring it to you."

"I'll take it to go," Noah answers, aggravation lacing his tone.

"Oh; you're leaving?" Summer inquires.

"Yeah; I've got some things to do," Noah says, looking into her eyes.

Summer gazes at him. She can tell his energy is off. She wonders what happened and if she can say anything to make him stay to at least enjoy the meal with her.

"Wow. I thought we all would eat together. When I feel better, everyone else is down. That sucks," she says, disappointed.

Noah chuckles. At that moment, Summer reminds him of his mom pouting when she can't get her way.

"Come on, let's eat," Noah tells her.

Summer eyes light up and a hug smile spreads across her face as she watches Noah cross over the kitchen and wash his hands at the sink. He grabs a napkin off the counter to dry his hands and takes a seat at the table. The two enjoy pepper steak with rice and a salad, lemonade, and small talk.

Chapter Seven:
SALVATION

"Ma, why do you keep staring at me?" Tink asks her mom with a smile.

They are sitting in the car in the church parking lot. It is a beautiful Sunday with the sun brightly shining, but the best part of the moment is her mother is a living testimony. They found out on Friday that the cancer in her uterus is gone.

"I'm so blessed. No one but God is responsible for this moment," her mom, Linda, replies, smiling.

Tink agrees with a head nod. Every time she'd thought about the possibility of losing her mom, she had teared up and cried. She had given her mother hell growing up, and she can only thank God that He didn't take her before she could make her mom proud.

"Mia died at thirty-three, and Aunt Pam is in a hospital bed waiting for God to give her the okay to come home. But me and you, mother and daughter, are here together, ready to worship the Lord together. I prayed for all of this," Linda says through her tears. She shakes her head. "Nobody but God."

"I prayed that you would turn away from the life you were living before it was too late. I prayed that you would no longer bind yourself with toxic relationships and that you would see your self-worth. I prayed that God would remove the cancer, not because I was scared to die, not because I was scared to leave you here alone, but so you could witness the goodness of the Lord." She looked up to the heavens. "Thank You, Jesus."

Tink wipes the tears that have fallen from her eyes down her face. She is so grateful her mother has beaten cancer. She does not know what she would have done without her here. If it weren't for God proving that He is listening to her by healing her mom, she knows she would be with Winter, who is currently on a mission to snatch a bag.

"I love you. Thank you for the prayers, Mom." Tink looks up to the heavens. "Thank You, Jesus. I will forever serve You and share with the world how good You are," she confesses.

Just a week ago, Tink was plotting her next come-up. She is a girl who sets up guys and robs them. She has been in the game since that first lick she, Winter, and their friend Asia hit together. It is the thrill and not having to work hard to get it that fed her desire. But, now, she is done with that lifestyle, and since Winter is pregnant, she wants her to be done too. They have already lost Asia. They should have woken up then, but they did not.

"Keep praying for her, she will come," Linda says, placing her hand on her daughter's lap.

Tink looks up at her. "Wow. How did you know I was thinking about her?"

"The Holy Spirit, *and* she called you twice and you sent it to voicemail. You almost always answer her calls, am I right?"

"Yeah."

Tink nods her head. She thinks about what her mother said, and she is going to pray for Winter until she comes to church.

"Ma, let's pray for her now."

Linda takes her daughter's hand and begins to pray.

As they walk into the church, all she can think about is Winter. She prays she will change her mind about hitting that house. Yeah, old boy is a square, but her gut is telling her something is off. Tink and her mother are discussing where to go eat after church when a familiar face catches her eye.

"Don't I know you?" Tink says, a little too loud.

They are in the hallway of the church. Her mother looks in the direction her daughter is facing; then with a raised brow, she looks back at her child, wondering how she knows the pastor's son.

Bazz looks at the woman he is chatting with, then back at Tink. When he remembers who she is, he smiles because he has not stopped thinking about her friend who had bumped into him. He excuses himself from the woman and strolls over to Tink.

"Yeah. How is your friend doing?" He is only asking to be polite, because knowing she is pregnant, he sure is not trying to holla. So, why can't he stop thinking about her? He has plenty of women.

"Ohhh..." Tink teases. "Let me find out you crushing on my girl..." Tink looks at her mother, then back at Bazz. "This is my mother, Ms. Linda."

"I apologize," he says, hugging Linda. "It's nice to meet you both. I am Bazz, and my father is the pastor." He extends his hand to Tink, and she shakes it.

'A pastor's son, huh? I know you are a bad boy; you can't hide it. Wow, wait until I tell Winter the pastor's son is a thug and he asked about her.'

"My friend is well. I will tell her you asked about her. You want to leave me your number?"

"Nah, I will see her around. You ladies take care."

Bazz walks back over to finish the conversation he and the woman were having before Tink interrupted. Tink and her mother continue on into the church.

"You know she has a man," Ms. Linda whispers.

Tink shrugs. Noah is cool, but there is something about him that doesn't make her comfortable when it comes to him and her friend being one.

Chapter Eight:
CAPTIVE

Winter pulls into the store parking lot, turns her car off, lays her head back on the seat, and stares off into the sky. It is a beautiful day, but for her, everything seems dark and gloomy. Winter's head feels like it is going to explode. She cannot stop playing the last twenty-four hours in her head. She cannot sleep, has not eaten, and has barely drunk anything.

'This is crazy. I can't believe it... The pastor? What-in-the-heck was he doing there? I hope he ain't no rat. Why did I let him live?'

Winter rubs her hands down her face. She wants to tell Tink, but she does not trust her with this. She isn't sharing what went down with anyone; it is too risky. She wishes the situation would just disappear, but with the way life has handled her all these years, she knows it is just a matter of time before things hit the fan. Besides, someone is dead.

Her jaws begin to fill up with saliva, making her stomach turn. Winter hurriedly opens the car door and spits out the liquid in her mouth. She then grabs a mint from her purse and puts it in her mouth. She doesn't feel up to moving, but she needs to hurry in the store because the suspense is only adding to her stress. Winter grabs her things and exits the vehicle. She makes it her business to be in and out of the store without being seen by anyone she knows.

"I promise it will get better," the deep voice offers.

Winter looks up and is shocked to see the guy she bumped into last week in the restaurant. He was walking into the store as she was coming out. Her heart feels like it will pop out her chest remembering what she has in her hand. Winter looks down at the brown bag she is holding, then back up at Bazz.

Being they are at a drug store and the way she is acting, Bazz assumes her nervousness has something to do with the statement her friend made that day: "Friend, you pregnant?"

"Are you okay?" Bazz asks.

"If I say I'm not, what will you do?" she sasses. "Gon somewhere with that; I'm not interested," she spits. At the same time though, she is thinking how handsome and chocolate he is.

"I would say, give it to God, because I can't do anything. They way you're looking, you have more issues than I do, and I've got some stuff going on." Bazz shakes his head, then he shrugs. "I'm just saying..." With that, he strolls off.

Adding to Winter's insecurities.

Bazz walks into the store and pulls his vibrating cellphone from his pants. When he sees the number, his stomach drops. It is his pops calling from the burner phone he gave him Saturday night. '*DID THE FEDS COME?*'

He then wonders what reason his dad had for not coming to church on Sunday. He knows something is off; that's why he has not gone by there.

Bazz walks out the store, down the sidewalk, and into the parking lot, making sure to keep his distance from the cars and patrons. With the Feds, you never know who they are. They will pose as a homeless person, and some foolish person who thinks they know everything will have an entire phone conversation in front of them, not knowing they have just snitched on themselves. If he is going down, he isn't going out like that.

"S'up, Pops?" Bazz speaks. He inhales and quietly exhales.

"I called the McGuires." He pauses and Bazz can hear the frustration in his father's voice. "Take this address down. You tell him everything."

"Yes, sir," Bazz replies, biting his bottom lip.

Bazz feels bad, not because his lifestyle has caught up to him, but because his dad is upset. He does not want to stress him, but he does want to do his own thing—and he has for four years. Now, he is low-key questioning if it was worth it: the house, the car, the jewelry, the envy? Everything comes at a price.

"Dad, I'm grown. I got this; I know what I'm doing," he says cockily.

"Nig—" His dad catches himself. "Every criminal believes they know what they're doing. If they did, the jails wouldn't be overcrowded. If they did, kids would not be walking around here fatherless."

"I ain't got no kids, so that's on them dudes. And I ain't going to jail," Bazz rebuts.

"You think God is going to keep saving you?" He retorts.

His pops stomach turns, and all he can do is shake his head as his own question hits home. He knows for a fact that God *will* remove His hand. It recently happened to him.

"You said I've got favor; you said I'm protected." Bazz's response is more of a question than an answer.

"Jesus!" His pops shakes his head. "Only a fool would believe God will not remove His hand. You cannot keep living for the world, thinking you're good with God," he says, speaking to both himself and his son. The pastor is in hot water, and before he has to face his reality, which he knows will be soon, he wants to make sure his only boy is straight.

"Pops, I am going to be okay, trust me," Bazz affirms, but his father can hear the doubt in his voice.

"Pray for wisdom. Pray for it. You need it," his pops replies before ending the call.

The conversation he and his father had plays in his head the entire drive to the lawyer's office. *'I guess God removed His hand.'* Bazz has too much pride to even pray he makes it out of the situation he is in. He is just going to believe what his father has been telling him for years: His favor and grace are why he is covered.

Bazz pulls in front of the building, parks, and exits the whip. He calls his pops to let him know he has arrived, but he doesn't pick up. Before Bazz can ring the buzzer, he hears a man's voice coming through the intercom.

"Someone will be down."

Bazz nods his head as he glances to the left, a sudden calmness coming over him. No matter what he says or how old he gets, he needs his dad. Bazz nods at his dad's driver, who returns the gesture. Then a revelation hits him.

'Where did he come from? Is he a Fed?'

Bazz became paranoid about the new driver. It is like he just appeared out of nowhere, claiming the last driver is his uncle and he is taking over. He makes a mental note to get at his pops about what he knows about the driver.

The door opens and Bazz is greeted by security. An Asian man dressed in all black, his gun visible, and an earpiece in his left ear steps to the side and allows Bazz to enter..

"I'll take you up."

'He must handle some deep cases to have his spot here. And bruh is strapped. Pops be knowing some of everybody.'

The lawyer's office is a warehouse with major security all around. When they enter the office, his father turns, looks at him, and stands.

"Son, this is Noah McGuire, Sr."

McGuire stands and extends his hand. "Let's make it as quick as possible. I've got a pissed-off wife who requires my presence at a barbeque I didn't want to have." He chuckles.

Bazz looks at his pops and takes a deep breath as he takes a seat in front of the lawyer. The tension is thick. All three men have troubles they are praying will not catch up to them any time soon.

McGuire starts to speak, but what he sees on the camera alarms him.

"Are you being followed?" McGuire asks, looking from son to father, then back at Bazz

The duo quickly stand to their feet, rush to the other side of the desk, and look at the camera. Cops are everywhere—uniformed, undercovers, and a SWAT team. The three men stare in a daze as they wonder about their fate.

Chapter Nine:
OUTCAST

Summer and Winter are in the living room, preparing to head to Noah's barbeque, but Winter isn't feeling it. She does not care to be around his family, and she has situations that are causing her to stress even more. Noah's father is who doesn't mind making her feel uncomfortable. The mother seems cool, but Winter can sense she isn't one hundred. However, she know family gatherings mean a lot to her man; plus, Summer will be by her side. Just maybe the day will block out a few of her problems.

The robbery she did the previous Sunday went bad. She still does not know how her gun went off. The thought of that day alone causes worry to rush her like a tidal wave. It takes everything in her not to buckle and drop. Oh, how badly she wants to scream or even just disappear.

"Thanks for inviting me," Summer beams, looking at Winter. She is so excited she could dance. "What's the matter?" Sumner asks Winter, who looks bothered.

"A lot," Winter admits and flops down on the sofa.

"Well, you can tell me."

Summer wants to hurry to get to Noah's barbeque. She recently found out Noah's mom is the face behind L.A.'s top fashion school, a school she wants to attend but cannot afford it. She also learned Noah's father is a big-shot lawyer. Before, she had no idea of Noah's parents' profession. All she had known was they are well off. What-the-heck he is doing with Winter she will never understand.

Summer tries her best to hide her annoyance. *'You could've told me in the car,'* she thinks.

Summer is too anxious to leave to sit. Winter needs to hurry up. "Sooooo, tell me," she says, masking her annoyance.

"I'm pregnant," Winter blurts out and bursts into a loud sob.

"What?! Are you crazy?!" Summer shrieks. "You don't need a baby. You aren't stable!" she scolds, as if she is Winter's elder and she should know better.

Winter looks at Summer in shock. What she is saying may be true, but it is the way Summer said it. She didn't even notice that Winter did something she never does: show her weak side. She has never seen Winter cry!

Swiftly, Winter pulls herself together. She slipped when she allowed her emotions to take over; she was having a moment. Learning about the pregnancy and dealing with the worries of Sunday's incident are a lot to deal with at one time.

"Really? A baby? Oh my god. I assume it's Noah's..." Summer quipped, trying her best to contain her anger.

"Yes, it's his. You know I don't get down like that!"

'I can't believe the boy isn't using protection with her. He must have low self-esteem. Maybe she did voodoo on him, because there's no way! She can't cook. She has nothing going on for herself, and she isn't even cute. This is insane.'

"I hope you don't plan on keeping the baby," Summer remarks.

"I know I gotta get rid of it, but I'm scared. I thought I couldn't have kids. Because of the rapes, the doctor said I would never be able to bear a child. That's why I always said I didn't want any."

Winter's voice cracks, but she refuses to cry. She did enough of that in her childhood. The fact that she is pregnant is a blessing and a curse.

"The doctors said I would never get pregnant. I can't—I can't do this." Winter stands and exits the room.

Summer's heart threatens to bounce out her chest. She is angry and jealous. She looks around Winter's apartment and thinks, '*How can she have this nice place, a nice boyfriend, and money, and I have nothing? She's a criminal. I make my money the legit way. Here I am struggling, I may get kicked out of school because I can't afford it, and here she is, about to have a baby and be a part of a well-off family. She doesn't deserve it! What makes her so special?*'

Summer is so into her feelings she didn't even notice Winter has left the room. Summer's eyes begin to burn. She fights hard to keep her tears in check. It just is not fair. She is not a religious person, but she questions how it seems as though the bad folks are always getting ahead, leaving the innocent to suffer.

'I hate her! I hate Aunt Vee! I hate Cousin Kelly! I hate them all! I am way better than them, and that is why they are so envious of me.' She is silently having a temper tantrum.

"Summer! Summer!" Winter calls. She has to shake her to pull her from her thoughts.

"What?!" Summer snaps. She looks Winter in the eyes as hate consumes her. *'Arrrgggghhh!'* she silently growls, desperately wanting to attack.

'I hope you die! No, I don't. I hope you—ugh!'

"Summer, I love you. Thank you for being a true friend. I don't know what's going to happen, but I want you to have this…"

Winter raises a duffle bag, handing it toward Summer to accept.

"What's that?" she asks with a frown on her face.

"Money. Pay for your school and save. It's yours. You deserve a break. Now leave that job and focus on you," Winter explains sincerely.

Summer snatches the bag and looks in it. Her eyes light up upon seeing the neatly-stacked bills.

"Where did you get all this money?" She knows, but she wants to hear Winter say it.

Winter gawks at her, feeling like a little useless girl under Summer's gaze. Summer knows what she does for a living, so she isn't about to explain where the money came from.

"A thank you would be nice." Winter's nose flares. She is seconds away from snatching the bag back. Summer is acting a little too ungrateful for her liking.

Summer is about to let her mouth get her into a situation she isn't ready for. She quickly recants her decision to say what is on her mind.

'And this is why you do not need a child. You are a loser. Why do I need to say thank you, when you robbed some innocent person to get it? It isn't like she gave me her hard-earned money. Someone else worked for that money; it isn't even hers. Noah is a fool to love her. Doesn't he know she will bring his family down? Noah, your family doesn't deserve what you will put them through if you do not get rid of her! Don't worry, I'll help you, Noah.'

Summer manages to offer a generic smile. "Thanks, Winter. No one has ever done this for me before."

She drops the bag, strolls over to Winter, and holds out her arms. Winter smiles and the two hug.

'If only I had a knife...' Summer thinks.

It is a hot and beautiful day. The duo pull into the McGuires' estate, and Summer's mouth drops. The mansion is beautiful. She has fantasized about being a wealthy fashion designer all her life, living large without a care in the world. She looks at Winter, who is gazing out the passenger window. There is no way she deserves a life such as the one that can come with Noah being her child's father. Summer grabs her cell and takes a picture of herself. She saves it, then pulls up her memo app. Summer places the phone on her lap, face down.

"Winter, can I ask you something?" Summer asks as she puts the car in park and turns the car off.

Winter looks at her. "Yes."

"Did they ever find out why your parents were killed?"

Winter freezes. She isn't expecting that question. She hasn't talked about her parents in so long.

"Nah," she lies. She knows, she was there, but she will never tell.

"Winter, I'm your friend. I can tell by your reaction that you are not being truthful. A lot of things in our lives are because of what our parents did. Like, their mistakes are the reason we go through drama. It's sad but true. My mom had a nervous breakdown after my father passed," she half-lies. "Some children and even adults are suffering from the wounds their parents caused, generational curses." Summer will never tell a soul, but she is suffering too.

The girl's momma was crazy and killed her dad, then tried to kill her. Summer saved her life by running away. For weeks, she slept in vacant houses, until one day, when she was walking down the street, she was picked up by Children Services.

"When my father died, my mom died with him. Winter, be smart. You will not be the best mom for that baby. How could you be? We must make it right for our children. We are not ready."

She is so convincing that Winter feels sorry for both of them. Winter goes into a daze. When she found out the truth about her mother, she had wanted to share it with at least one person, but the shame and guilt would not allow her to.

'Summer is right. My baby is cursed in the womb.'

"Come on. There's Noah," Winter says, changing the subject and climbing out the car.

Noah isn't expecting to see his girl getting out the passenger side of her own whip. He smiles. Winter has his heart, and no matter what people say, she is a good person. He walks up to his girl and hugs her before placing a kiss on her lips.

"Thanks for coming," he says and kisses her again.

"I had to drag her out the bed," Summer giggles, "but we are here."

Noah chuckles, knowing it is true.

"Hey, Summer. I'm glad you joined her. I like your dress," Noah compliments.

Summer is wearing a pink maxi-dress, and Winter is wearing jean shorts and an oversized Tupac T-shirt.

"How were your new clients? Did they give you a hard time?" Noah asks, taking Winter by the hand. Noah believes Winter is a caregiver.

Summer does a double-take as she wonders if Noah really knows what his woman does to get her money.

'How were your clients?! Ha! He didn't compliment her. Of course not, who wears that,' Summer thinks, smirking.

Noah's parents watch the trio from the upper level of their home. The mother thinks the friend is cute, and she can tell the two girls are totally opposite. Winter is pretty to her too, but she just isn't a person she thinks is a match for her son. She is afraid she has some dark secrets that will surface and destroy her son and their family. However, she never has shown her son her true feelings about the girl. She has welcomed Winter. Her parents tried to force her to leave her husband, and it only pushed her closer. She cannot and will not risk that.

"She's beautiful," Mr. McGuire says. "She's perfect."

"What?"

"She's perfect. I can tell. I bet she's the smart one. She probably hangs with *that* girl because they are family or she doesn't have a choice. That's my son's wife. Watch," he says, referring to Summer.

Mrs. McGuire chuckles. Most times when he calls things, they turn out to be true. Whatever his reason for declaring the stranger to be his future daughter-in-law, she goes with it. Some things she just doesn't question.

"Honey, I want you to find out why Winter's parents were killed and if they found the murderer."

"Ohhh, *now*, I have your permission to be in their business," he counters sarcastically.

"Yes; now find out." She turns and stands on her tiptoes, and the couple kiss. "Let's go greet the guests. Everyone should be arriving soon."

Winter is happy. Summer seems to be enjoying herself with Noah's mom and aunt. However, the dad is giving her death stares almost the entire time. Winter does not know how much longer she can ignore him.

"Hey, Winter, come help us in the kitchen," Noah's mom calls out.

"Winter hates the kitchen," Summer butts in.

"Well, we will fix that," Noah's aunt on his dad's side chimes in. "Noah loves to eat, and I know you want to keep him fed."

She smiles at Winter because she likes Winter. She is a girl who has been through some things, just like she and her brother. Her brother just has forgotten where he came from.

"Ha-ha-ha!" Mr. McGuire chuckles.

Noah gives his dad the side-eye. He stands and grabs Winter, who is sitting next to him, by the hand.

"Come on; I'll walk you."

Noah and Winter follow the trio into the house.

"Oh wow, look. Breaking news," Noah's mom says, looking at the TV in the second dining room.

Everyone stops and turns toward the television. Winter wants to faint when she sees the breaking news:

"FAMOUS PASTOR BOOKED ON MURDER. WITNESSES SAY THERE WAS AN ACCOMPLICE, BUT WE DON'T KNOW HOW TRUE THAT IS."

"I don't feel well. I need to go," Winter mutters, trying her best to control her breathing.

Summer hears her and cuts her eyes; she is pissed.

Winter is feeling dizzy. "Noah, I need to go," she whispers.

ॐ ◆ ॐ

Flashback...

"James, it's almost two years, and we are still here. Like, how long am I supposed to be the other woman?" the lady fusses. "Do you love me or her? Answer me!"

"If I can't get peace while I'm here, then I'm leaving." James replies.

"I think it's best. I'm forty-six years old, and I've been playing the other woman for ten *years too long. James, I'm done. There are men out here who would love to flaunt me. In fact, I have been seeing someone and I think I like him. The only thing getting in the way of giving him a chance is my love for you, but that will change today."*

"How dare you!" he seethes.

"Get your hands—" the woman cries, but her words are cut short.

Winter is standing on the other side of the door, confused. Who-the-heck is James? The dude whose house she ran into is named Barak, and he does not have the voice of an older man.

Winter had met Barak a few nights before at a bar. He was her mark, but he'd thought he had one when she agreed to go back to his condo. She went as far as to kiss him one time, then she made him stop.

"I'm on my period, but I promise the next time I gotchu. For now, I just want to enjoy your company. You are a good dude, and I like your style."

"Dang, you had me ready. Call a friend or something?"

"You gotta pay," Winter had replied, licking her lips.

She had watched as he walked over to his wet bar and focused on a portrait of a red rose. He removed the picture, revealing a safe. She watched as he typed in 4-22-4. 'Stupid,' she thought.

He opened the secret safe and pulled out two stacks of money, causing Winter to bite her bottom lip. She stared at him lustfully, thinking, 'I scored. He's an easy mark and I could rob him tonight, but I will have patience.'

Winter had sipped with him, pretending to wait for her girls to pull up. She had not called anyone. After a while, she told him her friends must have flaked but promised to make it up to him. He was too drunk to protest. Winter left, knowing she would be back Sunday morning, since the dude had said he would be at church.

Barak wasn't from Cali. He claimed to be from the Midwest, but he was on the west coast on business. The condo is his property for his comfort when he's in town.

'So, who-the-heck are the people in the other room?'

She had to get in there; that's where the money was.

'Just leave and try again; you're already outnumbered,' Voice one suggested.

Her ego chimed in, 'Girl, you've been doing this since you were a kid,' which was true.

After the first lick she, Asia, and Tink had hit, she had not looked back. Being a setup chick is her profession—just like it had been her mom's. It is so easy that she doesn't see getting money any other way at the moment. She plans to stop soon, she just doesn't know when.

Winter puts the ski mask over her face. With her gun aimed and finger on the trigger, she rushes into the room.

"HELL-NAH!" she yelps.

There in the bed is Tink's pastor from TV with a younger woman. His hands are around her neck and he is choking her.

"You think I'll let you leave me? I'll kill you!" he is growling.

"Don't move, or I'll blow your brains out, Pastor!"

They make eye contact. He notices the gun in her hand, but he is so mad at his mistress that it takes a minute for it to register what is going on.

Winter reaches into her back pocket and pulls out cuffs, holding them up. "Put these on."

She tosses them at him. Reluctantly, he removes his hands from around the woman's neck, and she drops like a rag doll. Pastor grabs the cuffs and puts them on frontward. Winter's eyes are glued to the woman, who isn't moving,

"Tell me she's asleep. Did you kill her?" Winter mutters.

Pastor looks at his mistress' lifeless body, and his eyes explode from fear when he realizes what he has done. Panicked, he jumps from the bed.

POW!

Winter's gun goes off. Pastor's hand goes to his abdomen, and he hunches over in pain.

"YOU SHOT ME!"

Winter's first thought is to leave, but she runs to the safe instead, removes the picture, and quickly enters the same code Barak used that night. There is so much money, she doesn't have enough room in her bag. She spots an empty black designer bag on the floor, and ignoring the pastor's cry for help, she stuffs the bag with the remaining money.

"Don't leave me! Take me with you. I can't be found here!" he begs.

"Hell no! Have you lost your mind?!" Winter counters.

"Please!"

Looking at the blood and the dead body, Winter begins to panic. Then the smell... She is done. She snatches off her mask and *throws up. When she is done, she looks up and the pastor is staring at her.*

"Don't worry. I'll have someone clean it all up. Just help me get dressed. I'm losing a lot of blood. Both of our lives are in danger."

She doesn't know why, but suddenly, she feels that it is in her best interests to help the pastor. Once he is dressed, they leave through the garage. She panics again and runs off, leaving him to figure it out.

"And that's why I don't go to church. There's always drama," Noah's mom is saying.

"Girl, everyone acts like church folks are perfect. We all have issues." The aunt looks at the TV and shakes her head.

"**The pastor was shot, and the owner of the home said his money was stolen. It is suspected the accomplice took off with the money. Is this the case of a bad deal gone wrong? We will have more tonight at ten.**"

EVERY ACTION HAS A REACTION...

Chapter Ten:
GOD'S MERCY

Sitting in the cell, all Pastor James can think about is how he messed up. He knew that at some point his infidelities would catch up to him. He also knew he could not break the heart of the woman—his wife—God had blessed him with and God would be okay with it. Over the last ten years, he has preached how man may write their story one way, but God will flip it to His will—and boy did God do His will.

Murder! He never would have thought he would go down for killing his mistress. He has no one to blame but himself. That is why he is contemplating if he will tell who shot him and robbed his mistress' nephew. His heart is leading to giving her grace, but she did rob a man. He is sure it wasn't her first time and probably won't be her last.

Pastor had gotten too comfortable in his position as one of the most sought-out pastors in California. Pastor James went from seeking God diligently and fearing Him to making an idol of himself. His years in the ministry, combined with the power to heal, deliver, and hear from God concerning His people, had gone to his head. His congregation is over five hundred in person, with thousands on the Worship Network tuning in on Sundays and Wednesdays. Fame had caused him to slack. He had stopped his one-on-one with the Lord and even elected to have his wife handle Bible study. God had told him when he first started the ministry what was required: stay faithful. If one thing James knew, he knew to obey God or be rebuked.

Sitting in the cell on the hard floor with his hand against the wall, he looked up to the heavens and shed tears for his mistress and because he had hurt the church and his family.

"God, I repent. Please don't stop using me for Your people. My flesh got the best of me, but my heart is for the people. Jesus, I'm sorry," he whimpers. "Father, God do not turn Your face from me. I am not coming to You as pastor, I am coming to You as Your son, James. Forgive me and forgive my church." James is bawling so hard, he can't stop even if he had wanted.

The two other men in the cell look on, shaking their heads. Even they know not to play with the Lord, and they don't even know Him like that.

Pastor James prays and calls out to the Lord until he feels comforted. He is close to drifting off to sleep when he hears a voice in his ear.

"There's no perfect person, only a perfect God. Your wife was a gift to you. You hurt her; she's Mine too. You are forgiven. Now go save souls for the rest of your life in prison. My people need you there too. Your light isn't dim. Even the warden will know you are one of Mine."

James begins to weep, not because of the revelation of his sentence, but because he is still loved by God. "THANK YOU, FATHER GOD!" he shouts at the top of his lungs.

Shortly after his encounter with God, he rises to his feet. A guard is approaching the cell.

"Pastor, you've made bail. I'm going to take you out the back way. The media is all over the place."

James nods his head.

"I've let your lawyer know already."

When the cell door opens, James walks out. He looks behind him at the two men, who are staring at him.

"God loves you. He would be happy if you went to church with your parents this Sunday. Apologize to them and let the pastor pray for you. Join the church and never stop worshipping God. Only then will all the charges be dropped."

"Amen," says the guard.

He looks at the men, who are staring in awe. "If I were you, I would listen. This man hears from God," the guard offers.

"Thank you," one of the young men says.

"We will go," the other co-signs.

As the officer escorts the pastor, he takes the opportunity to say what is on his mind. "We all make mistakes, but we all don't learn from them. I'm praying for you. This too shall pass."

"Thanks, my brother. May God answer your prayers of the last seven years. You shall have a child. It's a girl. Name her Hope."

The guard shouts. "GLORY HALLELUJAH. THANK YOU, JESUS!" He drops to his knees and looks to the heavens. "God, I give You all the praise. I ask that You have mercy on Your son. May Pastor James be free."

Although he might never be free to walk the streets again, he is free of his sin. God has forgiven him.

Chapter Eleven:
FOLLOW JESUS

"Momma, what kind of church you got me going to?" Tink asks her mother, who is fixing their plates.

The pastor's scandal has been blasted for the last two days on every channel. Her mom sets their plates of chicken and shrimp alfredo on the table and looks at her daughter.

"The church that God placed us in. No one is perfect. We all make mistakes. If we didn't, there wouldn't have been a need for God to send Jesus to Earth to bear our sins. I am not saying what they say the pastor did is right. It is wrong, and that is why he has been exposed. However, we cannot judge. IF—I know he did, but IF—he repented and we still hold it against him, we create an issue with God."

Her mother's concept sounds logical, but she still has mixed emotions. They said he killed his mistress, and that is insane to her. He cheated and he is a murderer. How could a so-called man of God do such a thing?

Chapter Twelve:
THOU SHALL NOT JUDGE

Summer is ecstatic and nervous at the same time. She is sitting in a five-star restaurant about to have lunch with Mrs. McGuire, the GOAT in the fashion industry. Last week, at the barbeque, they had hit off quite well. Shortly after, Winter had wanted to leave, which had pissed her off, but she had played it cool. She had left her number on a Post-It and prayed she would reach out to her. After all, they seemed to have more of a connection than she and Winter. It didn't take much discernment to tell Noah's parents didn't care for Winter. One, the Mrs. didn't say much to Winter, and two, she would catch the Mr. frowning at her. It was safe to say, the three of them were on the same page: Get rid of Winter, because she was too hood for Noah. She would be his downfall.

All week, Summer has been trying to figure out how she can link up with her idol, so the phone call and invite by Mrs. McGuire was a surprise. It is perfect. Summer can smell the same elegant, sweet perfume Mrs. McGuire wore at the barbeque. As the woman approaches the table, Summer bounces to her feet and bows.

"I noticed your mannerisms at my home. I like that. A girl with class will go far. Noah said you are a fan."

"Yes, I love you. I love your story. I—"

"Please sit." Mrs. McGuire extends a hand toward the seat Summer was sitting in when she walked up.

Summer quickly takes her seat, as does Mrs. McGuire.

"I'm so excited to be here with you. I never thought I would have this opportunity."

Mrs. McGuire smiles, thinking how she has Summer just where she wants her. She doesn't waste any time testing her loyalty to Winter.

"Who knows what will transpire after this meeting." She stares Summer directly in the eyes. "I've come to talk about Winter Santiago. Are you willing to tell me what I need to know about her?"

Without hesitation, Summer nods her head. "Yes. Everything. Winter isn't who your son thinks she is," she offers.

Summers declaration is a surprise but appreciated. However, she knows the girl can't be trusted. Anyone who will call someone friend and betray them is a snake that will bite anyone they see as a threat.

'If you ever cross me, you will die slowly!' Mrs. McGuire thinks as she stares Summer in the eyes.

A chill runs up Summers spine as she studies Mrs. McGuire's facial expression.

Tink scans the menu, trying to decide what she wants to eat. Her mind is on love. It is something she wants desperately, to experience true love. A man to love her who isn't ashamed to let the world know. Her last boyfriend drained her. He is nothing less than a narcissist. He is self-centered, a liar, a manipulator, and always the victim. Everything always was her fault. Thank God he went to jail, and this time, she isn't taking him back. She has promised herself that she will wait on God to send her mate.

"Hello," the waiter greets.

"Hello," Tink replies as she watches the waiter pour water from the thick glass pitcher into her glass.

It is a beautiful Thursday evening, and on this day, Tink decided to treat herself to a lovely meal at an elegant restaurant. Enjoying her own company is something she has promised to practice at least once a week, whether it be going to the park and enjoying a good book, a day at the spa, a walk on the beach talking with God, or a nice meal at a five-star restaurant as she is doing today. Tink is claiming the life God ordained of peace, love, hope, and joy.

Tink's eyes land on the pair sitting across the way. It is Summer and a woman who looks to be well-established. Who is she dining with? She didn't think the girl even had any friends outside of Winter. She is weird. Winter may be blind, but Tink can see right through the chick. She knows Summer thinks she is better than them, but she is a fake. Tink can sense it.

When the waiter walks away, Tink picks up her cellphone and takes a picture of Summer and the Asian woman.

'I just don't trust her.'

Tink has no idea who the woman is, but she knows Summer is up to something.

Chapter Thirteen:
JESUS IS THE LIVING GOD

Every minute of the hour, Winter is thinking about her next move and what life is going to hit her with next, which has led to her standing in front of a window that reads:

PALM READING
A PSYCHIC WITH SOLUTIONS

She always has wondered if it is real, and she made up her mind to find out. She needs to know if the pastor is going to snitch or take what he did to the chin. She doesn't have time to watch her back every minute of the day. She needs to find out what is going on.

"Don't go in there. You think you've got issues now..." a female voice says from behind her.

Winter looks behind her, and there stands a tall, slim woman who resembles her foster mother, the one she had liked so much. The woman is her twin and she is shocked.

"I don't know what you are going through, but those folks bring bad spirits that only God can break the hold that will be on you. Take your problems to God, not a witch doctor. If you have never listened to a stranger, listen now. Don't go in there, opening portals and summoning demons you are not ready to handle or have the power to defeat. The spiritual world is not to be played with!"

Winter doesn't say a word. She doesn't know the woman, so she has no response; however, she does take what she said into consideration. The woman looks away from Winter to a guy she has noticed is staring at them. He is about fifty feet away.

"Do you know him? It's like he wants to get your attention."

Winter looks in the direction the woman is gesturing. Fear rushes her. The man staring at her looks like a cop. Then he does something that spooks her: He chuckles and strolls off. Winter looks back at the woman, but she has disappeared. She looks around and doesn't see her anywhere. Winter becomes anxious and she needs peace. She rushes through the door of the shop of the person the woman called a witch doctor. It is dark and gloomy. She shivers due to the coldness. Then she inhales a nice fragrance and it relaxes her.

"Welcome, Winter," the male voice greets her.

Winter watches as a midget walks from behind the curtain.

"How do you know my name?" she asks.

The midget laughs. "Come, beautiful. I have all the answers you need."

"Wait. I am not sure if I can take what you are going to tell me at the moment, but I need to know. If it's okay, will you write it on a piece of paper, so I can read it later?"

The palm reader stares into her eyes, but Winter looks away.

"Sure, but make sure you read it before midnight. What I am going to tell you will save your life."

Winter gives him a head nod and follows him behind the curtain. An unction prods her to turn around and look out the window. There is the woman again. She looks at Winter with disappointment, or is it with pity? Her stomach balls up.

'*Don't do it,*' Winter is thinking as she quickly turns back and trails behind the man.

∾ ♦ ∾

A Few Hours Later...

"I'll take these and these," Winter says to the sales clerk in Nordstrom.

When the woman walks away, she flops down in a chair and blows as hard as she can. If only she could blow herself into another reality. The life she has she wouldn't wish on her worst enemy. She isn't the type to dwell on her troubles, but at that moment, she cannot help but wonder why God even brought her into the world. As a little girl, she was content, she would even say happy, but as she had gotten older, she realized she was experiencing more than she should.

Her mother and father argued often. They would call each other names and even fought. The police had come to her house so much she had stopped being afraid of them. Her parents had their good days, when they would hang out and eat dinner together as a family, but she remembered the bad days more than anything.

Then, there was that night... the night her parents had been killed. She would never forget what the man had said before pulling the trigger on her mom:

"She's wicked and she deserves to die. You don't need her in your life. My own sister set me up. Them-niggas killed Momma because of you."

POW!

The vision of the bullet in her mom's forehead was permanent. That was the last time she had seen her uncle, and she didn't know if he was dead or alive. As a kid, her uncle wasn't around much, but when he did come, she remembered he would come in big fancy cars, wearing big chains and rings on every finger. He would bring her lots of toys and clothes. When he would leave, she wouldn't see him for a while.

Sometimes, she hated him for killing her parents. Then, there were the times she longed for family and wished he was there. Maybe he cared for her, because when he killed her parents, he could have killed her too. Maybe the hope of him loving her was the reason she had never told who the killer was. Many nights, she would pray for him to come get her, but he had never come. Eventually, she acted as if he was dead, like everyone else.

From a little girl, Winter had become accustomed to the nightmares witnessing her parents' murder had brought. She had concluded they would never go away. On the outside looking in, it looked like she had it all together, like she was strong, but internally, she was suffering from the many hits of life.

The day the cops found her and her parents, there was an officer who had said to her, "Never forget, there are angels who are protecting you and a God in heaven who loves you. Pray and talk to Him when you are sad." Then he had handed her over to Child Protective Services.

She had tried it—talking to God and believing in angels a few times—but prayer had done nothing for her. The angels had not protected her from the uncle who had assaulted her. Nor from the mean adults who had talked down to her. God nor the angels were concerned with her, so she did what she did—took care of herself.

Now she is pregnant. Pregnant by a man who doesn't even know her. As much as she loves Noah, she doesn't think he loves her back as much. Not because he doesn't show it, because he does, but because they were two different humans who come from different backgrounds. What he feels for her would pass. She believes he is just infatuated with dating a tough girl.

Her mother had set men up and robbed them; her father had been her mother's pimp. One of her uncle had been a pervert. Her other uncle had killed his own sister. Her grandmother was the scum of the earth. Winter could not escape the sins of those responsible for her existence, if there really was such thing.

A tear falls from her eye as she thinks about the child in her belly. She thinks about the last robbery she did and her fate. She hopes she will receive some good news in the reading. Baby or not, she isn't trying to go to prison. She and Tink's childhood friend Asia had been caught up on a kidnapping and robbery charge. They had given her twenty years. Whenever they talked, she would cry and complain about how hard prison was. A year into her sentence, she killed herself. Asia was one of the most courageous people she had ever known. For her to give up, she knew it had to be a lot to deal with.

Winter sighs; she hates being a thinker. It is hard not to reply to the chain of events in life that are making her suffer. That is why she didn't smoke: She thinks too much.

"I have your shoes, Miss," the saleswoman announces as she approaches Winter. She holds out the box containing the wheat-colored Timberlands.

"You know what, I'm sorry, I don't want them."

Winter stands, grabs her bags, and proceeds to walk off. She can feel herself getting aggravated. Winter is a walking timebomb.

"PRAYER CHANGES THINGS," the saleswoman yells.

Winter turns, looks back at her, and offers a warm smile.

The saleswoman thinks, *'Whatever is on this girl is heavy.'* She can feel it.

"Prayer only works for certain people," Winter counters and walks off.

By the time Winter leaves the mall, she is hungry and tired. All she wants to do is go home, and if possible, hide out in her room forever. She tosses the bags in her trunk and gets in her car. Her ringtone lets her know Noah is calling. She cannot keep dodging him; it isn't fair. She takes a deep, calming breath and lets it out.

"Hey," she answers, trying her best to sound like she is in control, but that is *far* from the truth.

Winter's ear is glued to the phone as she waits for him to trip on her about how she has been pushing him away.

"Come to Steven's Ranch. I'm here now. We need to talk."

Winter can feel her heart in her throat. Her stomach begins to do butterflies. *'He's finally breaking up with me. I knew it was coming, but gosh, now? I don't think I can take it.'* Her anxiety is trying to get the best of her, but she refuses to fold.

"Okay; I'm on my way."

"Good," he says and ends the call.

"ARRRGGGHHH!" she screams. She is so tired of everything. "Why does life have to be so difficult, especially when I didn't ask to be here?!"

She chuckles, knowing she won't get an answer. Without warning, every bad thing that has happened to her and what could happen rushes her like five sumo wrestlers, knocking the wind out of her. Winter lays her head on the steering wheel and sobs. Years of hurt pour from the depths of her soul. Winter slings the car door open and throws her body out, vomiting. She hasn't even eaten, but it seems like she cannot stop. Her stomach begins to cramp as she manages to get out the car, walk near the back, and continue to vomit.

The fiasco probably doesn't last more than two minutes, but it feels like forever. She stands up, shaking her head and wiping her mouth. A ting pierces her heart, and as if it were an activation of love, her heart changes and her thoughts shift from, *'I can't have this baby,'* to *'I love this baby.'* Winter begins to doubt what she is feeling and even her thoughts.

'I will tell Noah,' she thinks.

Then she hears Summer's voice, *'You don't need a baby. You aren't stable! You'll leave that baby, and it'll suffer because of you.'*

Then she hears, "You will pour all the love you never received into that child."

She hears it loud and clear. It is so loud that she looks around to see if someone has actually spoken to her.

"You only want that baby so Noah will stay with you," another voice says.

Winter shakes her head. No, that isn't true. She will never use a child or beg a man to stay with her. That is one thing her childhood trauma has taught her: the gift of goodbye. It is what it is.

As Winter makes her way to the front of her car and opens the door, she feels like someone is watching her. She slowly turns her head and looks behind her. In unison, her eyes and heart flutter. There, sitting in a black-on-black Range Rover with his window rolled all the way down, is Bazz. They lock eyes, then he throws his head up and pulls off. Winter wonders how long he has been sitting there, what he witnessed, and what he is thinking of her. The last time they crossed paths, he hit her with a slick comment that had left her feeling that much more unconfident.

As if he can see her, she rolls her eyes. "Ugh! I can't stand him!"

A portrait of him flashes before her eyes. She hates to admit it, but he is fine and she could look at him all day. She shakes her head, thinking, *'Why do we keep crossing paths? Did he see me throwing up? I hope not. Why do I care?'*

Thirty Minutes Later...

Winter arrives at the park, finds a parking spot, and turns her car off. When she glances across the lot and sees Noah's black Ashton Martin truck, she gets butterflies. Her baby-daddy is about to break up with her. She shrugs. It is what it is.

Winter takes the personal bottle of mouthwash from her center console, undoes the top, and pours some in her mouth. She swishes it around her mouth a few times, then spits it into an empty water bottle before grabbing her purse and getting out. She sees Noah standing by the waterfall with his hands in his pockets. He offers her a smile and strolls her way. Her heart thumps a mile a minute. His eyes always light up when he sees her, but this time, not so much.

She takes a deep breath. "Hey," she greets him nervously.

"Hey," he replies, staring into her eyes.

Noah loves her deep grey eyes. Sometimes he thinks they are hypnotizing him into wanting to be near her so much. But her lips, her juicy lips, he could suck on those all day if she'd let him. He doesn't care what anyone says, Winter is sexy and her bad-girl disposition makes her that much more attractive to him.

He loves her, he loves everything about her. He'd once thought he was just infatuated with her because her looks and her style were so different from the girls he normally dated, but the more he spends time with her, the more he knows what he feels is not just a phase. He is not trying to be married and start a family any time soon, but he wants to chill with Winter for as long as she will allow him. Eventually, when the time is right, he wants to persuade her to go to school and major in something that will help her prosper in life. He is not knocking her, but he knows she is capable of much more than being a caregiver.

"Winter, do you know who I am? Do you know why I am with you?" he asks, taking her hands into his.

The question throws her and she frowns.

"Yeah. Do you know who I am?!" she snaps. She pulls her hands from his and takes a step backward.

He chuckles, making her uneasy. It is that cocky chuckle, the one that says, "I am all that and then some. I am above and not beneath. I am a king."

She doesn't like that. His being cocky intimidates her.

છે♦ન્જી

Flashback...

"So, you mean to tell me you don't know this word? Girl, you dumb-as-hell. Dumb!" her foster father insults her.

'I'd rather be dumb than be a fat midget. That's why all your friends make fun of you. Ugly!' Winter thinks.

Winter has been at her new location for two months. Her foster mom is beautiful and the nicest woman she knows, but her ugly husband, she hates. He is mean and always picking on her, but she has never told; she has learned her lesson.

"I bet you ain't going outside until your dumb self learns it."

Winter eyes water. It is Saturday morning and all the kids are going to the park to hang out, but Winter is forced to stay inside, learning words from the dictionary and their definitions. He is so mean to her, but he treats his grandkids and nieces nice.

"I'm trying to remember." She holds back tears. She hates for people to see her cry.

"HOW ARE YOU TRYING? I JUST TOLD YOU THE WORD TEN MINUTES AGO!" he yells, causing Winter to jump. "The only thing you have going for you are those eyes, and your hair is okay. I feel sorry for you. You ain't cute. Got those big lips. Don't even bathe until somebody tells you to. A real man, a man who's got something going for himself, ain't going to want you. He may sleep with you, but he ain't going to keep you."

By the time Winter is thirteen, she is already numb to the things adults say about her. If it isn't the guardians she is placed with talking about her and calling her names, it is their friends, the neighbors, and even some of the moms at the church.

Her time in that home is short. The mean man dies and his wife has a nervous breakdown. After the funeral, she is swept away with deeper insecurities than the ones she came with.

ॐ ◆ ॐ

So, when Noah asks her such a question, it rubs her the wrong way. He is a little too cocky for her. She knows it is just a matter of time before he shows his true colors.

"Don't look at me like that! You asked me do I know who you are, but do you know who I am?!" she snaps. "DO YOU?!" she yells.

Noah isn't offended by how she is getting at him. He knows she has misinterpreted what he meant. He takes one of her hands into his and places his other hand on her cheek.

"Yeah, I knew who you were when I first laid my eyes on you. I knew who you were when I pulled up on you at a group home. The night I got in your mess, I knew who you were. You are the girl I was attracted to the moment I laid eyes on her. You are the one who gave me a hard time to where I had to pay someone to steal your address. The one I had to have. And the one I got. The one I can't get enough of."

Winter blushes.

"You are the one I still want no matter what people think of us. Winter, I know you have been through some things, but I am not sure how much longer I can be okay with having only a piece of you. Did you believe me when I say I love you?"

She nods yes.

"I want your mind, body, and soul." He gazes into her deep grays. "It is required for us to continue."

She takes a deep breath. He is about to make her emotional. It isn't the first time he has confessed his love, but this time, he just doesn't know how much she needs to know that. Butterflies dance in her stomach as tingles travel through her body. She is in love too. Noah wipes the tears that are escaping from her eyes.

"Winter, I'm in love with you, and I know you love me too. But what I need to know is, who do you want? Am I the man you will share your pain with? It is the only way I can help you heal, but I gotta know if I'm wasting my time. Love should not be forced."

"Noah, I love you too!" she cries. "I'm pregnant with our baby. I know your family won't be happy, but I don't think I can get rid of my child," she blurts out through her tears. She doesn't know where the connection with the baby has rooted from, but she is no longer sure she has the courage to get rid of her baby. She watches him take it all in.

He cannot look at her. The news is a blow that has taken every breath he has in his body. His parents are going to flip. Noah releases her hand and takes a step back.

"Wow," he says, more to himself. He wasn't expecting that news. A baby? A father? Him?

Winter wipes the tears from her eyes. She knew it. That's why she holds back so much; it is to save herself from heartbreak. No one has ever stayed, and Noah is just like the rest of them. She turns and walks off.

"Winter," Noah calls after her, "come here." He jogs to catch up with her and takes her arm.

She yanks her arm back. "Look, I'm good. I've got to get away from here before I flip," she warns, never looking back at him.

"What did I do? What's the matter?"

"BOY, GO TO HELL!" she bellows.

Noah snatches her by the arm, turning her around to face him. He then pulls her into his arms and kisses her on the top of the head. Reluctantly, she buries her head in his chest and sobs. She is scared and feels all alone.

"I love you both, and even if we don't make it, I will never leave you to raise my child alone. That's *our* baby. I want it too, and thanks for telling me. I'm just shocked. I mean, this is big, but I would never turn my back on y'all. That's my seed, something we created, so whether we stay together or not, you two are my family. Whomever cannot accept you and this baby is rejecting me, and I will not stay or associate with those who do not respect me or my family. You having my baby means you are my family." He pauses, allowing Winter time to digest his confession.

"I won't lie and say I am ready for a kid, but I will never tell a woman to abort my child or leave my child's mother hanging. That's my word!"

Hearing him say this, Winter cannot help herself. She squeezes him so tightly that Noah can feel her love. He can also feel how fragile she is and knows he needs to have even more patience with her; after all, there is a baby involved.

"I'm scared, but I need this. I need my baby," she whispers.

"*Our* baby. He will always be *our* baby. You are not alone," he assures her.

Chapter Fourteen:
WISDOM OVER LOYALTY

"Girl, you'd better watch your mouth. You are doing too much!" Winter snaps, shutting Summer right up.

Summer places both hands on her hips. Winter is upset, but she is furious. The living room is full of tension so thick that it would take a chainsaw to cut through it. Summer stands there, ready to snap back. Ohhh, she wants to get at Winter so badly. She is raging like a bull, with smoke coming from her nose.

"Tell me how you really feel, because I'm starting to feel like you don't mess with me like I mess with you," Winter states. "And, if that's the case, you can bounce! I don't do fake!" She would never blow up on Summer, but Summer is coming at her like she is an enemy.

Summer can see that her statement has pissed Winter off, but so what? She means it, but this isn't the time to act on her emotions. She has to be strategic. She is not trying to fight the ghetto queen. Plus, she needs to stay at her place a little while longer. Summer places her left hand on her chest.

"All I said was, it's a stupid idea to keep a baby knowing your lifestyle. Winter, it isn't fair. I'm being honest. You rob people for money. Do you want your child to grow up unloved like we did? You know there is a possibility you will be caught. Remember your friend Asia killed herself?"

Winter's heart falls into her belly. What Summer is saying is true. Her past actions could lead to her baby being motherless, and she does not want that. She has every intention of leaving the life of a savage behind, but who is to say her past will not come back to haunt her as it did her mother? She had done so much in the streets, from Los Angeles to Las Vegas. On top of that, she still has the robbery involving the pastor hanging over her head.

"So, do I just kill my baby?" Her voice cracks. To protect her child's future, it seems best, but thinking about hurting her unborn child saddens her.

"I think it's best," Summer says with no remorse. She doesn't want kids, and she darn-sure doesn't want Winter to have a kid by Noah.

"Thanks for keeping it real. Thanks for not telling me what I want to hear." Winter grabs her fanny pack off the sofa next to her.

"Where are you going, to Noah's? Does he know?" Summer questions.

"Yeah; I wish I hadn't told him. He wants the baby," Winter says somberly.

"WHAT?!" Summer yelps.

Winter glares at her, puzzled by Summer's reaction. "Yeah, he wants our baby. He said he's got us," she let her know, her chest poked out with pride.

"Well, that's good to know," Summer lies. "At least he's a man, but we gotta be realistic, you know. If he knew about your lifestyle, he wouldn't want you to keep it."

Winter's eyes expand. She is trying to recall if she told Summer that Noah is ignorant of her lifestyle.

"Yeah, I know," Winter says somberly.

Summer cannot wait to call Noah's mom. She needs to know how foolish her son is being. *'He doesn't know who you are, but he will find out,'* Summer thinks.

"I'll be back later. I'm going to go get some air. I need some alone time," Winter announces.

"K; be safe." Summer clasps her hands together and offers a smile. "Everything will be okay. I'll be right by your side, and I'll make all the arrangements."

Winter offers a head nod and leaves the house.

As soon as she is gone, Summer grabs her cellphone and shoots Noah's mom a text asking if she is free. She paces the living room as she waits for a reply. She could have shut things down right then and there at the lunch she had with Noah's mom had she told her the truth about Winter Santiago: She robs people and she is pregnant by your son.

While at the restaurant, she had seen Tink when she was coming from the restroom. She was going to speak to feel her out but changed her mind, assuming Tink had not seen her. Winter had never admitted it, but she knew Tink was out there robbing people just as Winter was. She cannot stand Tink. She is a wannabe and always trying to get Winter to build a relationship with her mom, as if her momma is something special. In Summer's eyes, they are all low-lives.

A few hours ago, Summer had run into Winter when she was leaving that afternoon. Ironically, she had invited her out for a girls' day, but Summer had declined. She didn't want to be around the girl any more than she had to and couldn't wait to move out. Had she revealed all the awful things that followed Winter Santiago, there was no telling when Mrs. McGuire would have confronted Winter or told Noah how Winter was a piece of crap. She had to be smart and get her plan in order first. So, that day, she had kept her mouth shut, but now, she is ready to tell it all.

As she waits for Mrs. McGuire to text or call, Summer dials a number she has saved in her phone. It is to some condos she saw the other day when she attempted to see her aunt. Seeing her aunt hadn't gone well because she isn't on the visitors' list. She heard through her aunt's man that she had been back and forth in the hospital after the fight, but this last time, she had gone into a coma. Summer is heartbroken. Her cousin changed her number, and not knowing how she will react, she doesn't want to take any chances by just going to her house. It is all Winter's fault.

"Casa Park Living; how can I help you?" a cheery female voice greets her through the phone.

"Hello... I would like to view a vacancy, and hopefully, become a tenant," Summer responds.

Summer knows she is about to put Winter on blast, so she is going to have to get her own spot. The money Winter gifted her is twenty-five thousand dollars. She needs more, but it will do for now.

'*Why do you hate her so much?*' a shy-like voice invades her head.

'*Because people like her don't deserve to be happy. She's a loser,*' she replies.

KNOCK-KNOCK-KNOCK.

Summer jumps and her eyes focus on the door. "Who's there?"

"Detective Mason."

Summer eyes enlarge. She gently walks to the door, not sure if she should open it or not. Then a light bulb turns on: They are looking for Winter.

Chapter Fifteen:
PEACE BE STILL

Anger, annoyance, and frustration are his portion these days. He prays no one tries to step to him on some big, bad wolf madness. He isn't giving any passes, he isn't sparing anyone. He is going to lay them out and think nothing about it. That is on his mom, may she rest in peace. Bazz is a walking explosion.

Almost a month has gone by and Bazz has not spoken to his father. He loves his stepmom and respects her without a doubt, but he doesn't care what she says—he is done with his father. In his opinion, his pops is a fraud. If his stepmom wanted to forgive him and be by his side, that is on her. He doesn't have any words for him. How-in-the-hell does a pastor go down for killing his mistress?! It is lame. A weak move. He shouldn't have been cheating in the first place. His pops has a good woman, and he messed up for a piece-of-ass. Bazz is disgusted with his father.

Bazz pulls up to the Rink Apartments, located in the heart of Los Angeles. He parks in a lot reserved for the tenants, turns his car off, and pulls his blunt from the center console of his all-black Mercedes.

He sparks the blunt as he stares out the window at the dudes from his same set and chuckles. Just like his pops, there are a lot of fakes in the hood.

Some pretend to mess with him but talk about him behind his back. There are a few he had looked out for, but as soon as another hating homie offered to put them on, they had showed their true colors. They had acted like it wasn't because of him that their family ate, as if it wasn't because of him they had been able to make bail, or simply just put some dough in their pockets. He did a lot for his so-called homies, but half of them wouldn't even piss on him if he was on fire. The other half were users; they followed behind whomever had a bag and could help get them one.

Errybody by Mo3 and Boosie blared from the Bluetooth. The song is a whole vibe. Snakes and fakes taking over the earth, don't know who to trust. His stepmom frequently asked him why he even bothered to associate with the clowns in his old neighborhood, especially now, when he didn't know if the Feds were watching him or if he had been set up.

Bazz was born Bazar Tanner, the son of the famous pastor, James Tanner. Bazz' mother had died in a car accident when he was sixteen. She was the sweetest lady he had ever known, until his stepmom came into his life. Bazz isn't like the typical kids; he did not have daddy issues. His pops had been there for him all his life. That's what a lot of his so-called homies are mad about. They claimed he is a wannabe, that he had chosen the street life because it is fun—forgetting that, up until eight years ago, he had been raised in the same apartment complex they called the hood. Forgetting that his late uncles were from the set.

He had been around it. His pops could have tried to shield him, but he couldn't have blocked something he deeply wanted to be a part of. When his pops learned he had joined the gang, he had been angry and disappointed, but most of all, he had wanted to know why.

"Because it's where I grew up. When you were working, going to school, I was with my uncles, hanging out. It's me," he had replied.

It is that statement that had caused his father to do what he had to do to get them out of the hood. He had lost his twin brothers, cousins, and friends to gun violence; he wasn't going to lose his son. Shortly after Bazz confessed to his pops about being part of the hood, they had moved to

Conga Park, in some condos he later found out were owned by the church they had recently begun to attend.

Bazz hates everything about Conga Park. It is there he caught his first assault charge after beating up two white boys who thought it was cool to step to him on some racist crap. He had beat them with a chain. Had it not been for someone in the church representing him, he would have gotten time in jail. That time, he only had gotten probation.

His homies from the hood started insinuating that his pops worked for the police because he always got off when facing time. Them speaking ill of his pops had gotten him into some fights too. It was when his pops introduced him to the pastor's daughter, now his stepmom, that clarified why the church was doing so much for their family. His father was dating the pastor's daughter and being trained to be the next pastor of the church. Bazz was upset about it. He felt his dad should have talked it over with him before taking on such a strong position. And not just any church, but a church that is famous all over the country.

"Son, I love you, but if you can't respect what I have going on, you can go," his father had said.

And he had. Bazz moved out, and three months later caught a gun charge. He didn't call his pops; he took a deal before his pops even found out. Bazz served eighteen months in State prison. In jail, he'd linked up with a dude from Ohio. From there, he was put on to getting money as a scammer, something that had gotten him plenty of money, but now he has to slow down because something is off.

About two months ago, Bazz left his homeboy's birthday party faded. He wasn't trying to take that hour drive back to the house, and since he didn't have a chick with him, he decided to crash at his spot. His spot was an apartment in the city of Carson. When old boy from Ohio put him on to credit card and check fraud, he told him it was best to get a spot to handle all his work. And since he was going to make it a nine-to-five, he'd rolled with getting the place to set up shop.

That night, he'd pulled up. The complex was quiet, but this night, he saw the neighbors looking out the window. When he made eye contact with a couple of them, some of them shut their blinds or just stared. Being that his head was already gone off the Don Julio, he didn't even try to figure out what the issue was.

Bazz walked in his place, kicked off his shoes, and turned the downstairs light on. He used the guest bathroom, then flipped the light on in his downstairs bedroom, which he used as an office. Bazz did not even notice that his entire lab was turned upside down, paperwork everywhere, file cabinets open, and documents gone until the next morning. His spot was a disaster.

His first thought was it looked like the police had been there, but there was no sign of forced entry. Pulling out his gun, he did a check around the house and the backyard. Once he felt it was clear, he went to his safe, sweating bullets. The money was still there. All he could think was his time there had run its course.

As the weeks went by, he was trying to determine if it was the cops or a homie who had broken into his home—a setup, of course, but by whom? But it could have been the Feds. Bazz had no choice but to wait it out.

"S'up, bro? Are you getting out the car?" a homey asks. He is a tall, lanky white boy with freckles. Up until two years ago, Bazz had never seen him in his life. The hood isn't the same; they let anybody in now.

"Nah," Bazz replies.

He is high and feels like being in his own lane. Plus, the weed has him looking at everybody as a suspect. He doesn't know if any of the niggas are working with the Feds or followed him and broken into his spot. The neighbors aren't talking, so he just has to wait it out. Bazz starts his car, ready to bounce.

"I'm about to roll," he tells the dude at his car, ready for him to move.

"You know Suave got caught for that murder," the dude offers.

"Don't know what you're talking about and don't care," Bazz replies in a nonchalant tone. "I'm about to go though."

He doesn't have a destination in mind but ends up at Top Golf. He doesn't know if he is high or what, but it is like all that are in the building are couples and family.

"Ah, hell-nah, that's her nigga."

He chuckles upon seeing old girl from the restaurant. He would've gone over and messed with her, but she is hugged up with some pretty boy. *'So that's who got her pregnant.'* Bazz thinks about the day he saw her throwing up in the mall parking lot.

Bazz chills for a couple of hours until the place closes. He looks for ol' girl as he is leaving, but she must have left. As Bazz strolls to his car, he feels like he is being watched. If it is the Feds, there is nothing he can do; anyone else, he is blasting. He has to get them before he gets got. Bazz uses his key fob to hit the locks on his car and climbs in. He shuts the door. But as he goes to press the 'start' button, a cold piece of steel is at the back of his head. He wonders how the person got in his back seat.

"I'll blow your brains out!" the deep voice warns. "Nigga, put your hands up."

Bazz does as he was ordered.

"I want your wallet, your jewelry, and your gun."

"Take it!" Bazz barks.

"Give it to me now!" He presses the gun harder into Bazz' skull.

"Nigga, take it!"

If Bazz has to guess, the nigga is a cupcake. Either way, he isn't giving up anything.

Ol' boy knows Bazz isn't to play with just by how he has challenged him. He knocks him over the head as hard as he can. Blood drips as Bazz' head hits the window; he is dazed. It takes three attempts for dude to snatch the chains off Bazz' neck. He leans over the seat and takes his wallet from the front pocket of his sweats. And to make sure the-nigga doesn't try anything, he takes the keys to his whip. The door opens and the cold wind hits Bazz in the face. He shakes his head to regain his focus, and through blurred vision, he sees ol' boy running through the parking lot.

Bazz grabs his gun from his waist, jumps out the car, aims at his target, and lets it go.

Pow! Pow Pow!

Dude drops like a sack of potatoes after several bullets pierce his back. Bazz jumps back in his car and tries to start the car, but it won't start. He fumbles through his cup holder for the keys, but nothing. Police officers swarmed through the lot so quickly that Bazz doesn't know how he got in the squad car.

る◆ぺ

In his prayer closet on his knees, Pastor James prays in the spirit to his Heavenly Father:

"Lord, please forgive me for the sins I have committed, known and unknown. Thank You for having mercy on me. Father, I know there is no negotiating with You. I am humble before You. I know my actions are part of the reason my son is rebellious. Lord, I beg of You to not remove Your hand from him.

"I command the enemy to loose him right now, in the name of Jesus. Loose him right now, satan. You will no longer destroy our kids. I detach him from my sins. I detach the young woman who shot me from her bloodline's sins."

"On my son and that young woman's behalf, I beg for grace. I beg of You, Lord, to give them another chance and for them to be used as vessels to save souls in Your name, to glorify You. I declare they are free, in Jesus' name. Amen."

Chapter Sixteen:
I Am My Sister's Keeper

Tink is sitting in a booth, waiting for Winter to arrive. Besides talking on the phone here and there, she has not spent any real time with her homegirl. She has missed her; more importantly, she wants to know how she is doing. Ashanti is playing in the background, and on the four televisions are different music videos playing with no sound. Tink scrolls on her phone on Facebook as she sings *Foolish* with Ashanti. It is the perfect song for her current dilemma.

"I will not go backward!" she declares, taking a sip from her cup.

Shake It Off comes on, and Tink chuckles. God is loud and clear if you will just listen. '*I ain't giving that man no more years,*' she thinks of her ex.

The waitress approaches the table, and Tink orders two lemonades. As the waitress turns to leave, Winter strolls up and smiles.

"You look cute," Tink compliments.

She is dressed in black leggings, a white tank, a black jean blazer, and Jordans.

"Thanks," Winter replies.

She then addresses the waitress. "I'd like a water and fries, and bring the fries right out," Winter orders, taking a seat in the booth.

Tink stands and walks over to Winter. "Get up and give me a hug."

Using her hands, Tink motions for her to stand up. Winter is a little taken aback. They don't do things like that, but she stands and Tink embraces her.

"Let me see." Tink steps back and places a hand on Winter's tummy.

"Stop! I'm not keeping it. I wish I hadn't told Noah. He's smothering me. I can't do anything without him wanting to know or help."

Noah has been by her side constantly ever since she told him she is with child. It feels good to be loved on, but she knows it is just a matter of time before things change for the bad.

Tink places a hand on her hip. "Why aren't you keeping it? We talked about this. And Noah has a right; it's his child too."

"I said what I said, and you offered an opinion. And don't worry about what me and Noah have got going on!" Winter snaps.

"So, because a scared little girl tells you that you don't need the baby, you listen? Wow! And you offered to tell me about Noah. As you told me about Summer and her dumb and selfish opinion."

When Winter told Tink about Summer's take on her being pregnant, Tink was pissed, but she did not address it then. Tink takes a seat back in the booth.

"I guess I can't ask you to help me get rid of the baby?" Winter inquires.

"Ask Summer!" Tink retorts, picking up her purse. "I'll get with you later."

Winter thinks Tink is playing until she walks off. Then she shrugs, thinking. *We ain't ever gotta talk.'*

Chapter Seventeen:
THE TRUTH SHALL SET YOU FREE

"Glory be to God!" Pastor James greets the congregation.

"Glory be to God!" most repeat in unison.

Pastor James kneels and the congregation follows. When he is done praying, he stands up and looks into the audience. *'I am going to miss my home,'* he thinks as people begin to clap and whistle.

"WE LOVE YOU PASTOR!" some yell.

"I love you all too."

He allows them to clap for a minute before raising his hand and instructing them to be seated.

"Seeing you all here is another perfect example of God's grace. We have a full house, and I know it isn't just my church family, but others who have come to show love. If the world can do it, then children of God sure better. The church isn't perfect, but God is and is always faithful. Amen!

"Even after all of my mess, my God is still with me. Remember, there is no perfect person, only a perfect God, and when we mess up, God is there to let us know we can get through all things through Christ Jesus who strengthens us.

"My God is the reason I don't have to walk in shame. As long as Jesus didn't disown me, I can get through the mess that I created. When Jesus went to the cross, He already knew the mistakes His people would make. I am forgiven, but it doesn't mean I am not being reprimanded by my Father. Can't nobody whoop me like He can. I will serve my time and..." He looks at his wife, who is sitting on the first row. "And give blessings to my wife as she waits on her new beginning."

Ohhhs and ahhhs can be heard and the church gives a standing ovation.

It grieves pastor to see his wife cry.

"Please, allow me..."

He steps off the podium, walks over in front of his wife, takes her by the hand, and looks into her eyes.

One cameraman squats next to him on one side and another on the other side.

"You are the best thing that has happened to me. When I lost my first wife, I wished I was in that car instead of her, but I had to shake that off because I had Bazar to raise. Then God sent me not just a wife who loved me, but one who helped me see that my calling to be a shepherd to God's people is very important. It is because of you that I know God loves me."

Pastor takes his three fingers and presses them on his eyes, trying to stop the tears.

His wife stands up, nodding her head and allowing her tears to fall. She loves the man before her, and even after the hurt and embarrassment, she still wants only the best for him. She still wants the church and everyone who has been blessed by him to see and understand, that despite his sin, he is a man who loves God's people. The soul and spirit are willing, but his flesh got weak. However, it cannot be denied that he has been chosen by God.

"It's all right, Pastor, let it out," she whispers. "And I forgive you," she says with boldness.

Pastor James breaks down. Most of the men come to embrace him as the choir begins to sing *Jireh* by Elevation Worship & Maverick City.

"Jireh, You are enough / I will be content in every circumstance..." Pastor James hums as he listens.

When the song is over, he returns to the podium and begins to preach on forgiving yourself and to never stop seeking Jesus. He goes on to explain how God is not far as most think, how the Holy Spirt is with us, and how once we truly grasp the fact that Jesus is with us, it is easier to overcome oppression, depression, rejection, and the desire to do ungodly things.

"The only way that will happen is if we seek God diligently. Get in His Word. Put something of God in your ear throughout the day, and praise and worship Him."

He ends by saying, "Keep my son in prayer. Pray that he will say yes to his calling."

ACROSS TOWN...

Chapter Eighteen:
THE PLOT OF THE ENEMY

"I can't believe this! I can't believe this!" Mrs. McGuire fumes.

Noah is standing in the foyer with his parents, with his hands in his pockets, as his mom scolds him about him getting Winter pregnant. His listens as his mom is going off on him, periodically glancing at his dad, who is sitting in his chair, drinking a glass of cognac and not saying a word. He does not have to speak; his cool demeanor and the look in his eyes speak volumes.

Noah knows his dad. He is furious and probably going to bring drama to his and Winter's lives, but he is ready. Yeah, he still lives with his parents, but he is a grown man, and like he was raised to do, he is putting his family before any and everybody, and that includes his mom and dad.

"She is trying to trap you. She is nothing but ghetto trash. I can't believe this. I do not want a grandchild with her blood!" his mom declares.

Noah squints his eyes and tilts his head to the side, thrown by her last statement. Taking a deep breath and letting it out, he responds. "Mom, that's something you cannot change, and you don't have to see our child. He will not be around people who hate him or his mom, and that's my word."

"Excuse me?"

His mother turns and walks up in his face. Her son is not coming at her as if her opinion doesn't matter. His entire life she has done what has been needed of her to make sure he beat the odds. He was deemed a failure the moment he was conceived because her family was not happy about her being with his father. Noah Sr. was once a bad boy, but Noah is *nothing* like his father once was. Her baby deserves nothing but the best, and Winter is far from it.

"Are you choosing *that savage* over me?" his mom asks, pointing at her chest.

Noah is unmoved by her drama, and her tears mean nothing compared to the tears Winter cried in fear of raising their child alone.

"Her name is Winter, and I'm choosing my child over *anyone! Always!*"

She slaps him upside the head, but Noah doesn't flinch.

"Are you stupid?! You are going to ruin your life." She hits him on the back and shoulder. "Are you on drugs? Did she put voodoo on you?"

"Mom, please stop hitting me and talking to me like that."

"Get your son before I hurt him!" she warns, looking at her husband.

"Look, we are having our baby, and if you want to be part of his life, *of my life*, then you need to fix your issue with my decision and my woman." He pauses. "And how did you know she's pregnant?"

"My turn," his dad finally speaks. All eyes go to him. "I did my investigation," he states proudly.

"So, you're spying on her, invading our privacy? I don't need you all up in our business. That's crazy."

"Yeah, yeah," Mr. McGuire mocks as he sits back in his chair and crosses his legs. "Did you know your baby-mama is the product of a set-up hoodrat? A hoodrat who got her baby-daddy/pimp killed? The gold digger crossed the wrong person and now she's dead, but she left something behind."

He chuckles, stands up, and walks up in his son's face. He is couple of inches taller than Noah, so he has to look up. Although the revelation perks his interest, he keeps his cool.

"Apples don't fall far from the tree. Your baby-mama also is a professional thief, a set-up whore," Mr. McGuire proudly announces.

"Watch your mouth," Noah flexes.

"Son, did you know all this?" his mother asks.

"Nah, he didn't know." His dad chuckles.

He hands Noah an envelope. "This will tell you all you need to know about your baby-mommy. If you allow my grandchild to have a mama like that, we will cut you off and take the baby, so either way Winter will not have access to my grandchild. I can make things happen, but you know that, so do not try me!" his father warns.

"WHO-THE-HELL DO YOU THINK YOU ARE?" Noah yells. YOU BOTH ARE HYPOCRITES. FAKE AND PHONY! YOU'RE A THIEF TOO!" he yells, looking at his mom.

His dad punches him in the mouth and blood leaks. Noah stumbles back and catches his balance. He holds his bloody mouth.

"If you run up, I'll drop you. Try me," his dad warns.

Mrs. McGuire runs between the two. "You see what is happening! She is destroying this family already."

Noah uses the end of his shirt to wipe his mouth as he looks from his mom to his dad.

"Stay-the-hell away from me and my family!"

He storms out the house, leaving the envelope behind.

The odometer is over ninety mph as Noah dips in and out of traffic, rage consuming his very being. His parents' discovery is scandalous, but at the end of the day, he needed to know and Winter has questions to answer. She has been lying all along: "A caregiver for a rich southern couple." Yeah, right!

Shaking his head, he thinks, 'You had me fooled.' Her parents' past wasn't something he would judge her about. No one's parents are perfect, not even his. His mom smuggles millions for politicians, something her father got her into doing. His dad was heavy in the dope game until he met his mom. When she got pregnant, his maternal grandfather threatened to kill him if he didn't go to law school and marry his daughter.

Even though he has no proof, but Noah knows his dad is still into illegal activities; that is why he has such a secluded office space. A warehouse with top-notch security is not common for a high-profile attorney.

He loves his parents, but they will not run his life. They may cut him off, but it will not hurt him. They are the ones who taught him to save for rainy days and how to invest. Noah will be a millionaire by the time he is twenty-five; he knows it for a fact.

The light is yellow. Noah presses on the gas. He needs to make it to Winter ASAP.

Hooonnnkkkk!

Just as he approaches the intersection, a car turns in front of him. He attempts to press on the brakes as his hand continues to smash on the horn.

Hooonnnkkkk!

BOOM!!

The impact between the two cars sounds like an explosion. One car is wrapped around a pole and the other on top of that car.

"IT'S ON FIRE!" someone yells.

Chapter Nineteen:
SHE STRIKES AGAIN

Summer walks past Winter's room with a frown on her face. She has heard her throwing up for the last hour and is beyond disgusted—not by her sickness, but because she still has not gotten rid of Noah's child. She already told Noah's parents what they need to know about the savage their son is plotting to have a baby with, so she is beyond inpatient; she is ready for the couple to be over with already. She can't take it.

It has been over a week since Detective Mason came by looking for Winter. He did not tell her what it was about, only to have Winter to reach out. However, Summer didn't relay the message. Each time she thinks about the visit, she crosses her fingers, hoping for Winter's fate.

Summer walks into the kitchen, goes in the fridge, and takes out shrimp and sausage. She has learned that Noah's favorite is Cajun pasta. Winter is allergic to shrimp, which means she and Noah will be able to enjoy dinner alone.

"Hey. Can you go to the store and get me crackers and soda water?" Winter asks, standing by the entry into the kitchen, dressed in Ethika shorts and an oversized T-shirt.

Summer rolls her eyes before turning around to face Winter. She looks like crap. Her hair is all over the place, her big lips dry, and her face pale.

"I can; give me a minute. You look horrible. I know you can't wait until this is over with," Summer says.

DING DONG.

"Must be Noah," Summer announces excitedly, heading toward the door.

"Hey!" Winter calls behind her.

Summer stops in her tracks and turns to face her.

"Who said Noah was coming?" she inquires. She did not invite him nor did he call.

"He called me about thirty minutes ago. He said you were not picking up, and he was on his way," Summer explains.

"Oh," Winter replies, walking over to the fridge.

Summer gives Winter the onceover before proceeding to the door. With a smile as big as the sun, she opens the door.

"Hey," she greets before recognizing the person in front of her is not Noah. It is Tink. "Winter isn't feeling well," she states just above a whisper.

"Girl, if you don't move out of my way!" Tink retorts.

"Who's that?" Winter asks.

"Me," Tink says as she brushes past Summer into the house.

She holds up two bags in her hand, full of different things she and her mom think Winter will need.

"I got you some stuff."

She smiles. She doesn't even have to guess. From Winter's pale face and messy hair, Tink knows she is still pregnant and that makes her happy. She and her mom have been praying.

Subconsciously, Winter pokes her lip out.

"Ahhh, friend, you sick?"

Tink sits the bags on the floor and rushes over to her. The last time the girls spoke, Tink walked out on her, and Winter didn't care, but her presence now is needed. Winter is happy she is there. Tink hugs her and begins rubbing her back.

"It's going to be okay. When's the last time you were outside?"

"Days," Winter answers, pulling back.

"I had a feeling. Go shower and put on something cool. I'll make you soup, and after you eat, we will go for a walk. Sunshine is good."

'*Good; y'all leave,*' thinks Summer as she heads back into the kitchen.

"Okay, but Noah is on his way," Winter informs Tink.

"Well, he can walk with us; we are all family," Tink says, offering a smile.

Winter shakes her head at Tink. She knows what Tink is doing, but she isn't even bothered by it. All she wants is to feel better. As Winter leaves to get herself together, she thinks about opening up to Tink, sharing her fears and desires. She is going to explain to Tink why she is having mixed emotions about giving birth. She still is contemplating if she should tell her about how she and her pastor crossed paths.

Tink is a lifesaver to Winter. An hour later, the girls are walking around the block for a second time. Noah has not shown up and did not answer when Winter called, so the girls went on without him. Surprisingly, Tink doesn't bring up her situation. They talk celebrity business, something Winter learned from Tink.

"I can't lie, I do feel much better. Wow," Winter admits.

"I know. My mom wanted to come also, but I know how you feel about people being at your house."

"You came. She is welcome before you are." Winter chuckles. "I love her."

"She loves you too, and she prays for you every day."

Winter thinks about the reading she got. She still hasn't opened the paper and read what is on it. She thinks about the physic telling her she needed to read it before twenty-four hours. Truth is, every time she gets ready to open it, fear paralyzes her, making her hold off. She doesn't know if she is more afraid of the truth or because of the woman who claimed she was going to see a witch doctor and it would curse her.

"What do you think about getting your palm read?"

Tink halts dead in her tracks as she looks at Winter with wide eyes and places a hand on her chest.

"Girl, that is not of God! I ain't messing around. That stuff releases bad luck. The only message I want is from God. Winter, come to church. Please do not go fooling around with those spirits you know nothing about. You know the Bible speaks prophetic messages."

Winter takes a deep breath, and Tink sees the uneasiness all in her face.

"Sis, did you go to one of those places?"

"Nope; just asking. And I do not want to go to church!"

Winter wants to talk about the pastor and his cheating, but she does not want to bring him up because it might activate something that might backfire. They continue their walk.

"Okay; you will come when you are ready. I hope soon, but girl, I gotta tell you. Franco, who's in a halfway house, won't stop calling."

Franco is her ex, an ex she knows she needs to stay far from.

"It's like, every time you get on the right road, someone wants to come and cause you to detour," Winter asserts.

"Detour does not mean end back up where you were. Detour simply means another route. If you go back, then that is what you wanted."

Winter shrugs. "True."

The girls talk about Tink's situation as they continue their stroll. There is no way she needs to let that narcissist back in her life.

"Winter, is that in front of your building?" Tink asks.

Winter is so nervous she feels like she is going to pee on herself. It looks like dozens of police cars and a swat truck are in front of her complex. Winter can feel it in her gut that they are there for her. Tink feels it too. She has done a lot of dirt with Winter, and more than likely, if they have come for Winter, they will want her too.

"Wanna run?" Tink whispers.

Winter thinks about the reading she has not opened. Had she opened the paper, she might have known what is up. Her entire life flashes before her:

Her parents' consistent fights. The nights she woke up home alone and slept in the closet until they came back because she was afraid to be alone. The time she watched her mom beat a woman with a baseball bat and blood had leaked from her head. Her watching her uncle pull the trigger on her mother and father. Being molested by her own uncle. Being belittled and talked about by adults. Her granny giving her away to the system. Her being labeled a savage.

"You'll be dead before you are twenty-one," she had heard so many of them say.

"You ain't going be nothing."

"No one will never want you!"

"You ain't worth nothing but sex."

"You are worthless!"

"You rob people. You don't need a baby."

"You're grimy just like your mama."

"If you think I'll let you be with my son, you are stupid!"

The replay of her trauma hits her with so much force that her head begins to ring. She places her hands over her ears.

"The pastor! The damn-pastor snitched!" Winter cries. "I should've killed him."

Tink is blown away by what Winter is saying, but she has no time to figure out what she is talking about.

"Let's go." Tink turns around and begins to speed-walk back the way they came from.

"FREEZE! DON'T MOVE! BOTH OF YOU, PUT YOUR HANDS UP!"

Winter hands fly up in the air, and her legs begin to feel weak. Everything around her is going in slow motion. The nausea feeling causes her mouth to fill up with saliva, and involuntarily, her hands fall.

"PUT YOUR HANDS BACK UP OR I'LL BLOW YOUR BRAINS OUT!" an officer yells.

Winter legs give out on her and she collapses to the ground.

"PUT THEM UP! PUT THEM UP!" several police officers yell.

"Oh, my gooood! Nooo!" Tink cries out. "Help her!"

She watches as several officers rush over to Winter.

"SHE'S PREGNANT! BE CAREFUL!" Tink yells, but her concern falls on deaf ears.

Tears roll down Tink's face. With her hands behind her head, she looks at Winter, and all she can do is pray for both of them. *'I know you are going to get me out of this, Lord,'* she thinks as she looks up to the heavens.

Winter is cuffed, yanked from the ground, and forcefully pushed to a squad car.

"You are under arrest for the murder," one officer states, "of Veann Robins."

Tink is shocked. Although she had a feeling that fight was going to come back to haunt Winter, she thought her prayers had prevented it. Tink keeps her hands up. She is not trying to be the victim of another racist cop who sees no value in a Black life. The cops begin to get back in their cars. She doesn't put her hands down until they all have pulled off. Then she pulls her cellphone from her sweat pocket and calls her mom.

"Moooom-myyy!" she cries.

Chapter Twenty:
STRONGHOLDS

It has been a couple of hours since the blow up the McGuires had with Noah. Mr. McGuire is able to get his wife to stop tripping off their son's behavior, but she still is distraught, thinking she has lost her only child over his love for a worthless female. She is very angry, and if Winter had been in her face, she would have kicked her-ass and knocked the baby out of her. Her husband assures her that he is going to make all of it go away and she believes him, but it doesn't stop her from being angry.

The couple's cellphones ring at the same time. Motherly intuition kicks in and she panics, sensing something has happened to Noah. She is relieved when she sees it is Summer calling.

"Mrs. McGuire," she answers.

"Hello. Hi. It's Summer."

"Hello; how can I help you?"

She can tell something is bothering the girl or maybe she wants something from her. Regardless, it isn't a good time.

"I—" Summer starts but is cut off.

"Summer, sweetie, now isn't a good time. As I promised, I will reach out to you next semester."

The day at the restaurant, Summer had offered information on Winter in exchange for a spot in the school she so desperately wants to attend. Betraying Winter is a two-way victory for her. Winter will be out of the picture and Summer will get to attend the famous fashion school.

"I was calling to give you heads up on Winter. Don't worry, the info is free."

Taken off-guard by her statement, she bats her eyelashes. "Oh really?" she replies, sarcasm oozing from her mouth.

"Yes. Winter was just arrested for my aunt's murder," she says excitedly. "You work fast."

CLICK.

Mrs. McGuire ends the call and drifts into a stupor. *'I'm going to have to get rid of Summer; she talks too much.'* Her Jimmy Choo heels click-clack across the wing as she walks into her husband's office.

"Honey, I guess God does listen to our prayers," she announces.

He is still on his own phone call, so she waits until he hangs up before continuing.

"I guess God does listen to my prayers. Summer just called and guess what? Winter was arrested for murder, Summer's aunt's murder. Problem solved." She pauses. "But what about the baby? Oh wow. Well, it's ours, whether we like it or not." She shrugs.

Mr. McGuire slowly stands from his chair. He looks at his wife, trying his best to get the words out that seem to be stuck in his throat.

"Did you hear what I said? What's the matter?" she asks nervously when he doesn't respond.

He opens and closes his mouth, takes a deep breath, and says, "We've got to get to the hospital. Our son..." He gets choked up.

"What?! What's the matter with Noah?" she asks in a panic.

"ARRRGGGHHH!" Mr. McGuire yells.

He knocks the papers off his desk, sending them flying across the room.

"HONEY, WHAT'S THE MATTER?! WHAT'S HAPPENED?!" she screams.

"Noah! We've gotta get to the hospital. I just got word he's at Centinela, and it's bad."

For most of the ride, the car is silent. Mrs. McGuire's mind is racing as she dips in and out of traffic to get to her son. When she looks over at her husband, he is staring in a daze with tears running down his face.

"My son is fine. My son is alive. My son will not die. My son is not dead. My son is well. My son is not hurt," she recites the positive affirmations. The heavier the unction that something terrible has happened to Noah, the louder she recites the affirmations. "MY SON IS WELL!"

"Honey, did your pastor friend turn himself in yet? Please call him or his wife and have them pray for Noah."

Mr. McGuire's head snaps toward her. "Pray to who?" He chuckles. "Honey, keep saying your affirmations. We will have better luck." He closes his eyes and begins to affirm himself.

Mrs. McGuire isn't religious; in fact, she doesn't believe at all, but for her son, she will try anything.

"God, if You hear me, please save my son," she whispers.

Mrs. McGuire pulls in front of the Emergency entrance, puts the car in park, and hops out, running at full speed through the double doors. Mr. McGuire grabs the key fob from the cup holder. Taking a deep breath to try to calm himself, he exits the car and shuts the door. He looks into the sky and shakes his head. There is no way his son is fighting for his life. He just isn't going to accept that.

After a little digging and bribing, he was able to get dirt on Winter and make arrangements to have her destroyed. Now, there is a possibility he will lose his own son. He doesn't believe in God, but he does believe in karma.

"Aye, sir, you can't park right here," a security officer calls from behind him.

Mr. McGuire is in a daze and does not hear him, but even if he had, he still wouldn't have moved the car. Upon entering the hospital, he spots his wife at the reception desk.

"I NEED TO KNOW WHAT'S GOING ON WITH MY SON!" she is yelling.

As Mr. McGuire makes his way over to his wife, the administrator who phoned him heads his way. Her lustful eyes fall on Mr. McGuire and she starts to run into his arms, but she quickly snaps back to reality. She is at work, they are in public, and his wife is there! She takes a deep breath, puts her game face on, and walks over to her good friend.

"Mr. McGuire, right this way."

Recognizing the voice, he looks at her, cuts his eyes and looks back for his wife, who is approaching.

"Take me to my son!" he demands, taking his wife's hand.

"Yes, of course," she replies.

Summer...

"Thank God," Summer mutters.

She tosses the last bag in and closes the car trunk. It is the cool of the night, and all the hype about the cops coming and arresting their neighbor has died down. Summer is making her escape in Winter's car. By the time Winter gets out of jail, she plans to be long gone. If Winter says anything about her taking the car, Summer will claim Winter gave her permission to use it. She climbs into the driver's seat and shuts the door.

Looking back at the apartment, she looks up the stairs at Winter's door. The door is slightly ajar, which she left like that on purpose. As far as she is concerned, the neighbors can wipe her out, but the main reason is so blame for the money missing will fall on someone other than herself. Summer has taken every dollar Winter has. She has decided to leave town for a little while and come back after Winter is sentenced.

She puts the car in reverse, but her chest caves in when the red, white, and blue lights flash behind her.

"FREAK!" she blurts out.

૭~◆~૭

Winter...

Winter shivers and the coldness of the room is almost unbearable. She has tried everything to get warm—blowing and rubbing her hands together, and at one point, she put them inside her shirt—but nothing had helped. It feels like her hands are about to fall off. Not only is it cold, but the lights are so bright, they have turned her headache into a throbbing migraine.

The air and the throbbing of her head enhance every emotion associated with her current situation. She is terrified for her and her unborn baby. She already knows there is no way possible she will be allowed to keep her baby in prison. Her child will be left with Noah and his parents. Her baby will grow up calling someone else Mommy. What if the woman Noah chooses is evil like the people whose care she was put in?

"MAN, I DON'T FEEL LIKE DOING THIS!" she yelled, becoming overwhelmed thinking about how long the process will take and how much time she could get. "I've got to get out of here and get rid of this baby," she mumbles.

Winter eyes expand and she freezes, trying to make sure she feels what she thinks she is feeling. Then the flutter resurfaces. It is the first stage of her baby moving. She places her cold hand on her flat tummy as the flutters continue. Tears roll down Winter's face as she realizes her baby is trying to communicate with her.

The doors of the integration room open. Winter does not bother to acknowledge the visitors. She continues looking straight ahead, discreetly moving her hand away from her tummy.

"Here," the female officer says, placing a cup in front of her. The warm steam from the cup feels good. It is hot chocolate, her favorite, but she refuses to touch it.

Detective Ross is a slim-thick Latina who cannot stand hood-chicks, especially the black ones. She favors the pop singer Jennifer Lopez when she acted in the movie *Enough*. She is ready to take Winter down.

Winter is cold, hungry, and thirsty, but she refuses to touch the cup. She doesn't trust any cops. Plus, the police know what they are doing. She isn't about to give them the pleasure of seeing her act desperate. She looks up at the female officer, then to her left at the male cop standing posted in the corner. He is the cool, quiet one. He resembles the rapper Ice Cube, mean-mug and all.

"I need to call my attorney," Winter says, looking back at the female detective.

Ross leans over the desk into Winter's face.

"You want to tell us why you decided to kill your friend's aunt? Like, why did you think you would get away with planning a murder? That's her aunt; you're just a person she met in foster care. Now your life is over. I saw you holding your belly. The cycle continues and your child will be motherless like you are!" she states harshly.

Her words tug at Winter's heart. Her tummy begins to quiver again and silently she whispers to the baby, "I will not bring you here to let you suffer. I promise!"

"I need my phone call and my attorney. Apart from that, we ain't got nothing to talk about!" Winter spits. Her anxiety is on ten, but she plays it off.

"That's okay, because we already know you were the mastermind behind the entire thing. Just like we know you orchestrated the murder of your uncle."

Caught off-guard by the statement, Winter squints her eyes at the detective. That happened like eleven years ago. How had they even tied that together?

"Yeah. We have been watching you for a long time," she lies.

"I need my phone call," Winter reiterates.

She thinks about the palm reading she had and regrets not obeying the reader's orders. All this possibly could have been prevented.

Chapter Twenty-One:
PROTECTION

"Her bail is eighty thousand. Mom, she is pregnant, and she can't be in there. I need to go to the house and see if I can find her money," Tink says to her mom.

Tink is pacing her mother's bedroom. She has not been able to calm down since the incident. She is worried about Winter.

"How do we know the money is at her house?"

Tink takes a seat on her mom's recliner. "The girl does not believe in banks."

"Well, let's just wait until she calls. I know she will call her boyfriend at least. You said he has money."

Tink sighs. The incident only happened a few hours ago, but a few hours too long for her friend to be in jail. She had known that fight was going to come back to hunt her.

"Why didn't they take Summer? She was involved too?" Tink questions.

"Who knows?" Linda replies.

"I still cannot believe she did not open the door. I just don't trust her."

Tink was so upset when the cops left that she had gone straight home. After she had taken a few minutes to calm down, she had asked her mom to go with her to see if Summer knew more about what was going on. When they got there, the girl hadn't let them in. Tink knew she was in there too; she had only been gone for thirty minutes or so. Summer doesn't have a car and she had intentionally refused to answer the phone.

"I do not trust that girl!" Tink declares.

"So, that's why we should wait for Winter to call before we go back over there. I don't trust her either."

Tink nods in agreement. If Summer is on some snake-mess, she is going to light her up and ask for forgiveness after. The phone rings and Tink rushes to grab it off the dresser. The caller ID reads "jail".

"It's her," she whispers nervously and presses the "accept" button.

"Hello."

"Hey. Is Summer okay? They won't tell me anything about her. Did they do her like they did me?" Winter blurts out.

Tink's lip curls. Here she is worried about Winter, and she's worried about her sneaky friend.

"Summer is still at the house. My mom and I went to talk to her, but she would not let us in."

"Wait—they didn't take her too?!" Winter asks, shocked.

"No."

Silence.

"Good. If you can tell her to bail me out, that'll be good. I know it's late, but I'm ready to get out. I am cold, hungry, tired, and all that. And I need a lawyer ASAP," Winter explains.

It seems as if her world is crumbling even more, but she refuses to fold. Even if old secrets are revealed, she isn't going to fold.

"I know. Me and mom will go now and deliver the message. You try calling her too. She is liable to ignore us again."

"Thank you, and call Noah. Never mind; Summer has his number. I'll tell her to call him."

"Oh, okay. Anything else?" Tink asked, feeling salty.

"Thanks, Tink. I appreciate you, and tell Moms to pray for me."

"I will. Call back in about an hour."

"Thanks again. If I don't call back, I will be sure to call you when I get out."

"Okay. Be safe, and we only talk when lawyers are present."

"Yup; they tried though, but let me go."

The girls end the call, and Tink says to her mother, "Mommy, let's go."

Linda wastes no time getting out of bed and rushing to get dressed. She loves Winter because her daughter loves her, and deep down, she knows she is a good girl who just has had no love and guidance. She is lost.

Back At The Hospital...

"I can't believe you. We thought you were dead. I almost died thinking I'd lost my son, and all you're worried about is that ratchet girl," Mrs. McGuire fusses.

She is highly upset with Noah. She dang-near lost her mind, worried about the extent of his injuries, and the darn boy isn't even concerned.

"The nerve of you!" she says.

She looks at her husband, who is still somewhat zoned out.

Mr. McGuire had received a call from the head of administration. Her sister, who is the ER Charge Nurse, had told her that Noah had come in and he wasn't looking to make it. Immediately, she had phoned Mr. McGuire on his personal line. When they arrived, she had escorted the couple to ICU, but before they walked into his room, the nurse in charge stopped them.

"There's swelling on the brain. We have him on life support. Prepare for the worst." Then the nurse walked away.

Mrs. McGuire had broken down, dropping to her knees. Mr. McGuire had begun to fight the air. He had gone as far as threatening to kill the driver responsible. It had taken a minute for them to pull themselves together.

"Come on, honey. He needs us." Mr. McGuire had lifted his wife from the floor.

Mrs. McGuire had been so distraught that her husband had to hold her up. She had taken baby steps to the room, making it take forever to get there. She just couldn't face it.

When they'd gotten into the room, the kid hooked up to the machines wasn't their Noah. All she could do was drop to her knees and thank God. She didn't even pray, but she thanked Him anyway. Her husband, on the other hand, had cussed out dang-near the entire floor and demanded he be taken to his son. Apart from a couple of bruises, Noah was fine, and he had the nerve to still have an attitude from the argument they'd had before he'd gotten into the accident.

"Are you going to let me use the phone? Never mind," Noah says, annoyed.

"AYE, NURSE. I NEED A PHONE IN HERE NOW!" he yells, getting up from the bed.

"What are you yelling at her for? Worry about yourself. You don't know if there's bleeding on the brain. Relax," his mom scolds. "You don't need to call her."

"He's dumb! Simple-ass can't call her anyway. The girl's in *jail* for murder!" Mr. McGuire blurts out.

Noah damn-near loses his cool, but he refuses to show any signs of weakness to his dad. Mrs. McGuire looks at her husband like he is an idiot. Why would he even tell him? Noah calmly swings his feet to the edge of the bed as the nurse walks in.

"Here's a phone. I'm sorry there wasn't one already in here," she says as she plugs the phone into the wall.

"Take this IV out and hand me whatever you have of mine. And I need the discharge papers ASAP, or I'm leaving without them!" Noah orders.

"Son, what is wrong with you?!" his mom cries. Her son has never acted so harshly with her. They are best friends.

"LET THE-NIGGA BE STUPID. LET'S GO! NOW!" Mr. McGuire bellows.

"I can't leave my son. Just go. We'll be there later."

"I am not going back to that house," Noah states.

"Leave his dumb-ass right here!" Mr. McGuire is fed up.

Noah chuckles. Once the IV is out, he is waiting for his personal items. The nurse returns with a grey jogging set.

"Your clothes were damaged. They are in the bag, along with your other personal items."

"I'm gone," his pops says and leaves.

His mother walks over to him, places her hands on top of his, and glares into his eyes, her heart bleeding.

"Baby, leave that girl alone. She isn't worth it."

"So, your grandchild ain't either?" he scolds, shooting daggers at her so powerful her heart breaks, knowing her and her husband's scandal is going to cause more damage between them. She has to fix it.

"Look, Son, I love you. I'm your mother. My job is to protect you, but I must trust that you are the man we raised you to be and you will do the right things. I'm sorry. I know you don't want to go home. Do you want to see about bailing Winter out?"

Part of what she is saying is true. She does not want to lose her son, but part of her is using manipulation tactics.

"Yeah," he answers, sliding on the clothes. "I need to go see about her and get her out. She is carrying my child." He looks up at his mom. "Your grandchild..."

"I'll have Larry handle it now."

She pulls her phone from her purse. First, she texts her husband.

Text: **LET'S HOLD OFF ON PLAN B.**

Husband: **SO HE'S BAILING HER OUT? AND WE'RE HELPING?**

Text: **YES. NO CHOICE. I DON'T WANNA LOSE MY SON.**

Husband: **DO WHAT YOU WANT BUT NEITHER HER NOR THAT BABY WILL BE A PART OF THIS FAMILY. PLAN B IT IS. NOW ERASE THIS THREAD. I DON'T WANT TO SEE ANYTHING ELSE ABOUT IT.**

Text: **I SAID HOLD OFF.**

Husband: **DELETE THIS THREAD AND DO NOT FORGET WHO THE HUSBAND IS.**

Mrs. McGuire begins to bite her bottom lip, something she does when she is nervous.

"What's up, Mom?" Noah asks. He knows something is bothering her.

She shakes her head. "Nothing. Praying that Larry will be able to help us. Hopefully she has a bail, but if she doesn't, we can get one."

She is laying it on thick, but she doesn't want it to blow up in her face. She loves her son too much. She cannot let him discover she is part of the reason he is hurting.

Noah appreciates his mom's seeming sincerity. "Thanks, Mom."

"Of course."

As they wait for the discharge papers, mother and son are in their own thoughts. Noah is trying to figure out how he got caught up with a woman like Winter. In jail for murder? Mrs. McGuire is still praying she and her husband's scandal won't cost them their child.

⊱◆⊰

Winter...

Winter sits in the cell, worried about herself, her baby, and Summer. She has called her twice and she didn't pick up. She has a strong feeling the cops doubled back and picked her up. Winter blames herself. She should have just left the girl home and gone on the mission solo. That way, Summer, who doesn't deserve any of these troubles, would be free.

"I just need to post bail. That's it. I'll figure out the rest later," Winter mumbles, looking up to the ceiling.

"SANTIAGO! LET'S GO! YOUR BAIL HAS BEEN POSTED!" a male officer bellows.

Winter jumps up. "Thank You, God." When the words leave her mouth, she is shocked she has even said them.

"Yeah; had to be God to have someone post a bail like that," the guard mocks.

The processing takes three hours. By that time, Winter is feeling sick. She has not eaten or drank anything since she got there. As she is being escorted out, her head begins to spin and she slows her pace.

"People run out of here. What's your problem?" the female guard asks.

"I feel faint," Winter mumbles as her heart rate begins to decrease.

"If you fall out in here, you gotta stay here to be treated. You only have a few more steps before you're out that door. I guarantee that you don't want to be treated here."

Winter gathers as much saliva as she can and swallows it. Taking slow breaths, she manages to make it to the door.

"Step aside!" orders the guard.

Winter leans against the wall as the doors open and the cool air gives her some relief.

"Be safe," the guard offers as Winter makes her way out through the steel doors. The brightness from the sun causes her to put her hands over her eyes.

Winter looks around for Summer, but instead her eyes fall on Mrs. McGuire. Instantly, her stomach balls into a knot, her heartbeat stops, and the dizziness increases. Beside her is Noah, wearing a scowl on his face. Why are they there? How do they know?

Winter takes two more steps and collapses.

Chapter Twenty-Two:
THE ATTACKS DON'T STOP

"Look, I told you, I'm afraid of her—I'm afraid of her, but at the same time, I needed her. When my aunt put me out, I had nowhere else to go. I know she's a bad person, but as long as I pretended I needed her, I knew she wouldn't hurt me. But if I went against her, I would probably be dead just like my aunt. She made me go. She even pulled a gun on me!" Summer cries, lying through her teeth.

Detective Morris is not moved. He knows she is full of it. He can spot a snake in a cotton field. The young woman in front of him is acting like a victim when she is far from it. He will not be surprised if it was her plan to act as a helpless human, so her friend would do her dirty work. But since Detective Ross made a side deal, he has to roll with her and ignore the fact that he knows Summer Edwards is lying through her teeth.

Detective Ross, on the other hand, is endorsing everything Summer says. In her opinion, Summer is beautiful, smart, and unfortunately, has been dealt a bad hand. Winter is the scum of the earth, and she is going to take her down—just as her good friend McGuire requested.

"Are you willing to testify in court?" Ross asks.

Summer eyes widen. She wasn't expecting to have to face Winter as she was plotting to end her life. She begins to bite her bottom lip and her left leg shakes uncontrollably.

"No, she isn't going to testify," says Morris as he pushes himself from the wall. He walks over to Summer and leans on the table, looking her directly in the eyes. "Are you willing to swear under oath?" He cannot take it, he hates her kind—a snake.

Morris makes her uncomfortable. Summer shifts her eyes to Ross.

"If I testify, will I be protected? Winter knows a lot of dangerous people."

"Yes, you will be protected. I can assure you, no one will harm our witness. It's time to get her off the streets. Are you willing to help?" Ross counters.

Summer swallows the lump in her throat.

"I am. I also have other information on her," Summer offers.

Ross nods her head. She pushes the notebook and pen in front of her. "Tell us everything."

Summer looks into Ross' eyes and nods her head. "Okay."

Chapter Twenty-Three:
WALKING IN SHAME

Winter lies in the hospital bed, pretending to be asleep. She can hear Noah and his mother talking to a Dr. Chang.

"She is eleven weeks pregnant, she is severely dehydrated, and her heart rate isn't where I would like it to be, but that little fella..." He pauses, looking at the baby monitor. "Has a strong heart rate, but mom must get well so he can stay that way." He looks at Winter with a warm smile.

Winter's heart flutters hearing the doctor talk about her baby. The room falls silent, and as if she has heard the sound before, Winter's ears perk and her heart swells, knowing that the thumping and swooshing sounds belong to her unborn child. They are the most beautiful things she has ever heard. The little person growing inside her, whom she hasn't even met, has stolen her heart. Tears seep through her closed eyes and run down her cheeks, confirming to her two unwanted guests that she is faking sleep.

"Mom, step out for a minute please. In fact, go on back home. I'll get a way home," Noah whispers.

"Okay, but call if you need me." She takes his hand in hers and looks her son in the eyes. "Don't allow your emotions to make you speak things you'll regret."

Mrs. McGuire leans up and kisses her son on the forehead. She then walks over to Winter and touches her on the shoulder. Winter keeps her eyes closed, but she knows it is Noah's mom.

"I'm here for you and the baby. We all make mistakes," she expresses.

One part of her is trying to show concern, just in case whatever her husband has up his sleeve backfires. If it comes down to it, she is going to blame everything on her husband; she plans to play dumb. She isn't losing her son. The other part of her feels sorry for Winter. Although she doesn't feel she is good enough for her son, she does hope she can overcome the things that are hindering her. She leaves, leaving Noah and Winter alone.

"Winter, I know you aren't sleeping. I need you to woman up and talk to me. Now ain't the time to be acting like a coward!" he states harshly.

Noah is angry. He even sounds like he no longer wants her. It is in his tone, and he has never called her out of her name.

"Why did you lie to me? Shouldn't I have a choice if I want to date a criminal or not? And now you're pregnant with my child!" He shakes his head.

Winter tries her best to conceal she is crying, but with the sniffling, coupled with her shaking uncontrollably, she is exposed.

"So, you ain't going to talk now?! You don't have anything to say? Winter, you are carrying my child! I HAVE A RIGHT TO KNOW ABOUT THE SAFETY OF MY CHILD!" he bellows. Noah is so loud, she thinks the windows might explode.

Her eyes open, her head snaps to the left, and she glares at him. He is being a little too territorial when it comes to their child.

"This is my child too!" she spews.

He chuckles. "I can't deny that, but *are you his mother?*"

"WHAT?!" she shrieks. Winter sits up in the bed. "Who do you think you are? Is *your momma* a mother?!" she snaps back.

Noah cuts his eyes at Winter. He turns around, crosses the room, and shuts the door. He makes his way back to Winter's bedside.

"You set dudes up. I can't have my baby around that," he speaks just above a whisper.

"YOU DON'T KNOW WHAT I DO!" Winter bellows. "THIS IS MY CHILD TOO!"

By now, her tears are flowing, but she doesn't care. Noah has made her angry acting if she is a bad mother. The baby isn't even born yet, and he has no right yelling at her as he is doing.

"I didn't know what you did to make money before because you lied to me, but you'd best believe, I know you are a thief, and like I said, I don't want my child around that. Winter, why? I could have helped you get a legit gig." With a disgusted look on his face, he tilts his head to the side. "What is it, do you think you are too good to be legit like the rest of us? Or you think you—" He stopped.

"I don't need you or anyone else. I'll give you back the bail money."

"I bet you've got it too!" he spits.

Then he chuckles. Noah wanted to believe it is all a lie, but his gut knows the real. The fact that Winter doesn't deny it only adds fuel to his already-blazing fire. He cares for Winter—loves her—but he isn't messing with a set-up chick.

"Noah, get out. You don't know anything. You don't know anything about me. Go back to your perfect world and I will stay in mine, a world where nothing was handed down to me. A world where, from the day I was born, I was covered in my parents' sin, making everyone count me out before I even had a chance!"

"Perfect world, you say?" He cracks a smile as he shakes his head. "Now you want me to feel sorry for you? You've had over two years to let me know what was going on in your life. You didn't even try to be honest when you told me about the baby. You are selfish. Does Summer know? I'll bet she doesn't. Tink knows, huh?"

"GET OUT!" she screams.

"I'm taking my baby!" he threatens.

"I'll kill this baby before I go nine months just to give her away!" Winter confesses. There isn't a smile on her face.

Noah walks up in Winter's space. "If you get an abortion, you may as well kill yourself, because I promise I'll make your life a living hell."

WHAP!

Winter's hand goes across his face, the force causing Noah's head to jerk to the side. His cheek is on fire, but he plays it off.

Winter jumps from the bed. "Get out, and that's my last time warning! GET OUT!" She is seething.

Winter forcefully wipes the tears from her face, using the back of her hand to wipe her nose. Winter glares at Noah. The way he has gotten at her crushes her, but it angers her more. All her life, people have made her feel like she is nothing, and now Noah is doing the same thing. The only difference is he had pretended to care about her. Yeah, she had lied, but nigga, tell me how you really feel. Is her thought.

Noah has never seen Winter so vulnerable; it is new to him. In all the time they have been together, this is what he has wanted: to see the softer side of her, the side that allows him to be a man. He would have comforted her and told her everything would be okay. That they are in this mess together, and he has her back until the wheels fall off.

But it is too late for all that now. She lied to him about who she is, had him falling for a straight thug, and on top of that, she is carrying his child. A child he wants no matter who the mother is. A child he is going to protect at all costs. If that means he has to keep him away from his own mother, that is how it will be.

"I bailed you out because you are carrying my child. I don't know if you are guilty of the charges brought against you, and it's really none of my business."

He goes closer to her. Winter's fists are balled up, and she is breathing heavy. Noah glares into her deep greys, desperately wanting to hug her, have her rest her head on his shoulder, and tell her they will get through this together. But, nah, she lied to him and had made him look like a fool in front of the people who wanted what they had to end.

"Look, you're carrying my child and that means we are family, so I ain't going nowhere until all this is figured out. But you and me are *done*," he expresses, meaning every word. You only have one time to play with Noah and it's a wrap.

"But I don't—"

Winter stops talking as two people enter the room. Her heart stops. She and Noah make eye contact. The lump formed in Winter's throat hurts. She closes her eyes and swallows. It feels like she has gulped down a golf ball. It hurts. Her mouth fills with saliva. It feels like she has to vomit. One second her body was hot and now cold. Everything is too much to handle. She thinks about making a dash for the door, but how far will she get before she is caught?

A voice whispers, "If God is with you, who can be against you and win?"

To Be Continued...

www.authoraletawilliams.com

Buy Now $8.00

https://square.link/u/KjCtcJWr

Made in United States
North Haven, CT
24 January 2024

47870939R00128